what's with baum?

SWIFT PRESS

This edition first published in Great Britain by Swift Press 2025
First published in the United States of America by Post Hill Press

1 3 5 7 9 8 6 4 2

Copyright © Woody Allen 2025

All rights reserved

The right of Woody Allen to be identified as the Author of this Work
has been asserted in accordance with the Copyright, Designs and
Patents Act 1988.

Interior design and composition by Greg Johnson, Textbook Perfect
Printed and bound in Great Britain by
CPI Group (UK) Ltd, Croydon CRO 4YY

A CIP catalogue record for this book is available from the British Library

We make every effort to make ensure our products are safe for the
purpose for which they are intended. Our authorised representative
in the EU for product safety is Easy Access System Europe, Mustamäe
tee 50, 10621 Tallinn, Estonia gpsr.requests@easproject.com

ISBN: 9781800756298
eISBN: 9781800756304

what's with baum?

a novel

by **woody allen**

Swift

To my amazing wife Soon-Yi.
Where did you learn that?

LATELY ASHER BAUM HAD BEGUN TALKING to himself. Not just the occasional mumbling of a man trying to clarify his thoughts or calm himself before some daunting task. Nor was he engaged in any delusional score settling with imaginary figures past or present. This would have made him bonkers or crackers which he was not. At least not yet full blown. That the conversations were a sign of early dementia was also ruled out as he was a fit fifty-one, with a sharp memory and no family history of any sort of cognitive gremlins. The only warnings from his doctors were to go easy on salt, use sunscreen and do just what he's been doing on the treadmill. If he suffered from anything, it was hypochondriacal panic attacks where he saw the abyss in every mole, cough and hangnail. And sadly, in every song, flower and rainbow. When Baum looked in the mirror, he recognized an intelligent mutt, a mixture of his father's sad eyes and his mother's Semitic nose and his own anxious contribution.

His hair, which was full but incoherent, and his Foster Grant black-rimmed glasses gave him a scholarly air. If he

1

were a movie actor he would have played shrinks, teachers, scientists or writers, the last of which is exactly what he was. In that same mirror he couldn't help noting a few silver strands debuting here and there and saw this as a sign not of the promise of wisdom but with his luck, an aluminum walker.

As the summer wound down, Baum took to strolling around the seventy-some acres of green lawn and wild woods that surrounded the large pond fronting his and Connie's country house, or more accurately Connie's country house, chatting himself up on deep themes. Circling the far end of the pond where the woods began, Baum would often find himself in an intense discussion on some pressing issue. Even in the house, if no one was around, he might strike up a conversation if he felt the need to communicate, to pour his heart out. After all, who else should I talk to? he reasoned. Who else is so friendly, so congenial and perceptive, so engaged and decent? Yes, decent and most important, understanding. Who else hears me out with an open mind and a little sympathy and cares? Does anyone give a damn that I'm constantly pushing a rock up a hill? And if I ever get it up there, then what the hell have I got? A rock on a hill. Great. So why am I struggling?

Lately Baum had gotten into more and more disagreements with himself. Some rather heated. Still, he thought, who but Asher Baum can grasp the magnitude of my suffering, the scope of my concerns? Who can I bitch to that wouldn't tune out after two minutes of my profoundest queries and not say, "Stop kvetching Asher, it's tiresome. We have our own problems." And yet all I'm trying to do is make lucid this minuscule slice of hysteria I routinely inhabit. Or no, maybe it's bigger than that. Maybe what I really want is to make sense of all people's lives. Of everything, the whole shebang.

Baum wanted in his writing to bring order to the chaos and tragic truth that seemed to cloud mankind's every sunrise. Long ago he had declared war on Auden's sound of distant thunder at the picnic. He believed he could best wage this battle with the human condition as a novelist by writing moving literature. These works must be great, he thought, because the night is large and the enemy is full of dirty tricks.

He decided early on he could not fight the fight as a mere journalist, reporting on the mundane ups and downs of reality. Fiction, he felt, was more real than reality, more capable of approaching the soul and getting to the truth of what the hell is going on. For Christ's sake, who's in charge here? He wanted his books to have an impact, to change people's perspective, and for that he needed to get the whole thing right. He did not want to march victim-like into eternity not having left behind at least a few volumes that helped ease the way for others. He was determined his tombstone should not read: Here Lies Asher Baum—So What?

He could no longer talk to his wife. Not about the things that mattered most to him. There's too much hostility with

Connie, too much anger, too much disappointment. No more patience with my complaining, he thought. Fourteen years that began with dinner dates and flowers had through the drip, drip, drip of broken dreams and things said that could not be taken back formed a critical mass, ready to detonate. She's five years younger than me, he figured. Still very beautiful, still desirable, still with that biting instinct for the jugular, which he once found so attractive. Of course, Dracula had a biting instinct for the jugular, but now it was Baum's. I guess in some ways I still love that complex thoroughbred, he thought, but I certainly can't talk to her. Not without quickly getting on her nerves. Nor can I talk to my brother Josh because he's sleeping with her. Or has once. Or I think he has. I'm not positive. I feel our conversations have grown stilted and while I love him, I do not trust him; and because I cannot reveal my suspicions as they would hurt him, we can't talk. I mean we can speak but not from the heart. Or at least not from my heart. Did I mention I think he slept with Connie? Yes, of course I just did. Great. All I need is to start repeating myself. That would be the icing on the cake. I also can't talk to my first wife, Nina. Too guilty. I was such a *meshugganah*, and she was so nice. My first signs of irrational behavior were with Nina.

Baum had married at twenty-one, anxious to move out of his parents' house and begin his life as a young newspaperman. He fell for a pretty Barnard student, Nina Glass, who happened to be an identical twin. Meanwhile, after two months of marriage he fell in love with the twin sister, Ann. Let's just say a Shakespearean comedy did not follow but what did caused Nina great suffering and Baum bewilderment, guilt and self-loathing. He talked it over with an analyst who sought the answer in Baum's dreams but what worked so well for Joseph and the Pharaoh didn't seem to click on that couch in the little room on East Sixty-Eighth. He didn't have any idea what had become of the Glass twins, but he knew if he ever saw either of them he would be too ashamed to speak. He had long ago given up talking with shrinks because in order for analysis to work the patient must be willing to change and the only change Baum was willing to make was the analyst.

He also could not talk to his second wife, Tyler. For one thing, she lived in New Zealand, but more important than distance, she had dumped Baum and gone off with some rock drummer who got very rich, very young, retired at thirty, bought a farm in Walter Peak Station and raised sheep. This came as a tremendous shock to Baum, and before that happened, he had only been to Payne Whitney as a visitor. He didn't even want to talk to Tyler or ever think about her except he did sometimes, particularly on rainy afternoons.

That was it. There was no one who really understood Asher Baum except Asher Baum. No shrink, no ex, no friend, as they all seemed to have fallen away over the years. No one who made any sense except the man himself.

Now he wandered across the lawn, reached into his pocket and took out the small antique box Connie bought him, which in earlier centuries had held snuff to make some fop sneeze. What fools these mortals be, he thought. Sneezing for pleasure. Now the box held Nexium to cure his reflux, a Xanax, one Ativan. All that was missing, he joked, was a cyanide capsule.

He popped the Nexium, having just completed his stroll around the far end of the pond where he had been in a heated discussion about the poor reception his last play received. A few times he had tried his hand at drama in makeshift theaters off Broadway and found it even harder than novels. Ponderous and didactic, the press had said. The same criticism he got on his novel. Moralizing they wrote. His conclusion was that criticism, no matter how beautifully written and full of elegant-sounding insights, always boiled down to mere opinion.

He was on a roll with his writing but sadly it was a roll downhill. His last book was pretty much panned and so was the one prior—about a man and a woman who fall in love in a concentration camp, manage to carry on a passionate affair, risk death and torture by secretly meeting over and over for three years, finally to be liberated whereupon she dumps him saying, "It was fun while it lasted but you're not really my type." The book garnered faint praise. Very few bothered to read it and amongst those, most failed to see the satire and lambasted it for making light of the Holocaust. That was the year he tried meditation but couldn't focus his mind on anything but his bad reviews.

Still smarting from the last conversation with himself about the demise of theater, Baum made his way back to the house, a pretty colonial style home authentically reproduced except for the large glass picture windows that would have delighted the Pilgrims if their decorator had thought of it. The windows afforded a generous view of the pond full of cute frogs and pan fish and the lovely Massachusetts woods full of red maple and black birch. Baum hated the country and much preferred the sight of the sun coming up each morning over Beekman Place to anything rural America had to offer. Still, now that the fall plantings were in full bloom, he had to admit that the asters and pansies and chrysanthemums were joyous to behold though still not as life-affirming as lox and bagels at Barney Greengrass. In winter, covered with snow, the scene might have been painted by Grandma Moses, a painter he loved despite her subject matter.

Baum had always hated the country, everything about it: the ticks and spiders; the raccoons, cute but with rabies; the poison ivy; the sound of crickets and cicadas. He hated the isolation and the ghostly silence and dead black of the night. Yes, a Constable landscape for real took one's breath away—for about six minutes. It was a great visit, but when the oohing and ahhing was over, it was back to civilization. Bookstores, record shops, cinemas. He enjoyed them even as they were almost all gone. But who wants to live where you need a flashlight to take a walk after dinner? True, the stars, unencumbered by Broadway's lights were a thing to behold, sparkling in their infinite multitude, but to Baum they were terrifying. These blazing spheres of hot gas, so immense, so distant. My god, the thought of those numbers, everything measured in light years. And the whole *megillah* with huge hunks of rock flying aimlessly amuck in pointless violence. What is going on up there? Beseech the stars as you will, they will never grant you a single wish no matter how modest the request. Baum thought the crime and violence of the city streets was *bupkis* compared to what was happening in the night sky. He recalled once in a store everyone standing by impotently as thieves brazenly helped themselves while the security guard stared frozen into the barrel of one of New York's ubiquitous Glocks. Still, in the city there's hope and one has options. There's people, there's police cars, Good Samaritans, and doormen. If you're isolated in a country house and a car pulls up at 3:00 a.m.—brother, that's all she wrote.

Of course, all these unsettling thoughts did not trouble his wife, Connie. She was protected from anxiety by a loving childhood, good looks, and high intelligence backed up by faith in "something greater" which Baum always said was her trust fund. Watching her cool down after her morning run—a beautiful creature, tall and haughty with white skin, jet-black hair, dark eyes. Think the wicked queen in *Snow White*, a nasty babe but hot.

"Thane is coming for the weekend, and he's bringing his girlfriend. I hope you're going to join in the conversation and not tune out. I love that he's serious about this girl."

"Did I ever meet her?"

"You didn't but I did. You would have if you'd have come to his book party."

"I was running a temperature."

"Bullshit. You're jealous of him but you could have sucked it up for one lousy hour."

"Connie, can we not—"

"It's okay—subject dropped. Anyhow, she's a lovely girl and of all the girls he's brought home, this is the one I'd love for him."

"Okay."

"And on Friday there's going to be a film crew up here. They're doing a feature on Thane and his book. It's caused such a sensation. Did I tell you it's already past the thirty-five thousand mark? You realize what that is for a first novel?"

"I was planning to get some writing done this weekend. Do we really need a TV crew here?"

"Stop grumbling. They may want to interview us, so think of some nice things to say. Force yourself. And stop telling people I have a blind spot when it comes to Thane and making your unfunny Jocasta jokes."

Connie. Constance. Connie and Thane. He loved the name Constance. It was so old-fashioned. Out of date in the freshest way. The raven-tressed eye candy of two unobservant

Beverly Hills Jews. Spoiled rotten of course. Daddy the big agent, Ben Lister, and Mom, the ex-movie actress, Holly Neal. Holly was a drop-dead gorgeous starlet who never made it. Eventually she got tired of being hit on by every casting director in town, threw in the towel and got her real-estate broker's license; she said goodbye to the movie business and sold French chateaux, Mexican adobes, and Italian villas all side by side right off Sunset Boulevard. Pushing rental homes once lived in by the likes of Clark Gable, Katharine Hepburn, maybe Esther Williams to twenty-one-year-old movie stars earning salaries with many zeroes brought in fat commissions. Peddling mansions was how she met Ben, selling him a home in Malibu with a swimming pool and tennis court.

Connie, an only child, grew up amidst the famous, kids with their theme birthday parties who watched first-run films in their parents' screening rooms, and she hated it. She chose to move east and go to school at Harvard. She married a very successful eye surgeon in Boston, a marriage that lasted four years. Next up was the architect Philip Dunn, a neurotic genius she met in London and spent years married to in the Cotswolds. Connie loved woods and fields, thatched roofs, gardens, and brilliant men. They had a child and when the scenic designer Damian Bass, a pal of the Dunns, suggested the name Thane, they loved it. They moved to New York where she had an affair with Damian Bass that broke up her marriage, and Dunn took his quirks and tics and moved back to London while she kept the country house they had purchased some miles from Great Barrington. She remained friends with her ex despite their breakup though they almost never saw each other anymore.

Connie had a pied-à-terre in Manhattan but spent most of her time in the country. She loved the thought of being a woman married to a creative force, living in a house covered by vines and roses with perhaps a salon in her study peopled every so often by fine minds and gifted souls. She thought she might have found this inspired artist with Baum when she first met him but that is not how things went. Still, if he was a disappointment to her, the Berkshires were not. She spent the days gardening, making jewelry and socializing with friends who had first or second homes around the Lenox-Stockbridge area. She raised Thane, a sensitive child with his father's colt-brown hair and patrician profile and his mother's nervous intensity and passive-aggressive charm. Connie adored Thane and in his eyes she was perfection. He would do anything to please her, to win her love which he already had but nevertheless reveled in winning it over and over.

And as she dated an assortment of interesting men, it was her son's precocious insights and youthful sophistication that commanded the biggest portion of her heart. She spoiled him as she had been spoiled, even more so as he was companionable, and she was skeptical about another marriage after two failed ones. She took Thane into the city, to films and plays, to museums and concerts. On their excursions they dined at high-end restaurants and had good chats and sometimes spoke French with each other. He loved nature in all its kaleidoscopic forms and photographed birds and had an ant farm. He read copiously, and his mother loved reading to him and for his tenth birthday bought him a hard copy edition of the *Encyclopedia Britannica* because it was so much more charming than the digital.

Connie, unlike Baum, had no qualms or jitters with time and space. She felt more than equal to the comets and shooting stars that scared the hell out of him and feared not the mysterious black hole that gobbled up a million suns a day, a statistic that could paralyze Baum should he pause to visualize it. One time someone gave her a magazine profile on Tadeusz Borowski that a journalist named Baum had written for a high-end intellectual quarterly. She found it brilliant, and it made her want to read Borowski's book, *This Way for the Gas, Ladies and Gentlemen*. For the only time in her life, she wrote a fan letter to Baum thanking him for making her aware of the author which Baum answered politely. In reply he had recommended several other Holocaust books including one he had written. She wrote and thanked him. It would be years before their paths crossed again but when they did, stuff happened.

Now Baum watched her disappear into the house and followed along. She went upstairs to shower, and he went into the kitchen to make a cheese sandwich. He cut a piece of

good Swiss from the wooden platter that had held the hors
d'oeuvres she had served last night when they had Damian
Bass over. Bass had long ago bought a place a few miles
from her house, and he and his wife, Nora, had encouraged
Connie and Dunn to consider the area around Tanglewood.
Baum worried that she had never gotten over her crush on
Damian Bass. She had cheated with him when she was married to Dunn so why not again? Damian had a new wife and
appeared to be calmer but retained his luster. Bass was a
great scenic designer, an artist by common consent and there
was her weakness for creative souls. Baum wondered if they
might not be occasionally canoodling behind a tree. They
were, after all, neighbors. It would be very convenient. And
intimacy between Connie and Baum had started to fall off
two years ago, and like any falling thing, it accelerated on
the way down.

"I think she's sleeping with Bass," he said aloud to himself.

"And I think you're going nuts." So went his one-man
conversation.

"I know. You're going to say I'm paranoid."

"You've actually gotten worse. First your brother Josh,
now Damian."

"What can I say, the marriage has deteriorated."

"Well sure. You haven't come through for her."

"Please—don't go there because you're liable to say
something you'll regret."

"She thought you were destined for great things. She thought she was hitching her wagon to a star. Y'know she has an ego too."

"Tell me about it."

"But you have not emerged."

"Because I won't settle. I set the bar high."

"You know what I say to that? Ha!"

"Okay, so inform me, wise guy, why my novels don't seem to move people."

"Can I speak frankly? Because you're trying too hard to be great. Your fiction is didactic. You want to change people's lives, impart wisdom. It's boring, Asher—you equate enjoyment with triviality."

"I am not a lightweight. There's too much inside me. I'm deep. Is that bad for an author? Tell that to the great Russian writers."

"You asked me. I'm trying to be straight with you. She thought she was marrying an artist. You have a modest gift and you talk a good game."

"You're really starting to get on my nerves. You don't know what the hell you're talking about. Meanwhile that little coddled egg, that Midwich Cuckoo, is called an artist because he sold thirty thousand books. Connie actually thinks he's going to win a Pulitzer."

"She's proud."

"Proud? She's orgasmic over what? Over a lousy bestseller?"

"And his reviews. And by all the high-brow critics. They talk about his depth and satire."

What's with Baum?

"I could never stand that kid. A spoiled, supercilious cockalorum with all the answers. And such arrogance— I should change my aftershave, he tells me. I should pick a less obnoxious fragrance because he's convinced that's what's causing his sinus problem. I couldn't stand that kid from the first night I met him years back when she dragged him to the New Year's party. The kid at nine in a little suit with his cocktail glass. Fuck him. He spilled his Shirley Temple on my jacket the first time we met. I wanted to kill him. Believe me, it was no accident."

"I'm sure he didn't do it on purpose."

"What the hell do you know? The kid hated me right off because he was worried I'd come between him and his mother. He sensed there were sparks between Connie and me, so he tilts his Shirley Temple on my tweed jacket and makes out like it's an accident."

"Thane, Connie and Damian Bass, your brother and Connie—listen to yourself. I think you snapped your cap."

"I'm telling you my brother knocked her off that night in the snowstorm."

"What proof do you have?"

"It's that you don't know Josh."

"My god, he's family. The two of you were close growing up."

"Yes, we were close but as we got older we grew apart. You just don't know him. Alone with a beautiful woman on a snowy night. For Christ's sake he'd screw a snake if you held its head. You think because we're brothers, because we grew up together, but we're polar opposites. He embraces life. He likes to hike and hunt. He has many women and I, I—"

"You're a schlemiel who's afraid of getting sucked into a black hole."

"I cannot embrace life. Sue me. To me it's a nasty business, and I'm not like Josh. He's a people person. I'm not. I have a dim view of my fellow man and I have six million bodies to prove it."

At that moment Connie poked her head out of the upstairs bathroom.

"Are you calling me?" she asked.

"No, no."

"You did that the other day. I saw you out the window across the pond. You were gesticulating like you were in a conversation."

"I was probably going through a new scene I was writing. I'm toying with another play. I'm not discouraged by those pretentious theater phonies."

"I'm sure it's not pleasant to get knocked but I told you when you told me the idea that it sounded turgid. But Jesus, Asher, don't talk to yourself. That's scary."

And with that she went back into the bathroom.

Baum felt guilty for his suspicions over his brother. Josh was a good man and loving brother, a great success in real estate. The fact was, Baum was hoping Josh would make another investment if he did another play, which he knew would be a hard sell given the money lost on his recent flop.

Also, the plot he was toying with based on the enforced starvation of five million Russians by Stalin and God's silence seemed less than a theater party favorite. Yet Baum was convinced those themes were the only ones worthy of putting time in on. He acknowledged people needed their escapist entertainment but that was not the purpose of great literature. Distraction from reality was better left to television and Hollywood. Certainly, Chaplin made Baum laugh but because his movies also showed pain the work struck deeper.

Connie came out of the bathroom showered and sparkling with her hair still wet, making her even more attractive. She put on jeans and a plaid shirt.

"I'm going into the city tomorrow or the next day. Just for the day," he told her. "Is there anything you need?"

"What's happening in New York?"

"I have a few meetings. I need to see Josh about something."

"What?"

"Oh, just some matter about our father's will. Can you believe it's been two years since he died? And my agent wants to talk with me."

"Scott? What does he want?"

"I don't know. He didn't want to get into it on the phone so of course I got a little concerned. He said it was nothing, but I know Scott Bell and whenever he lapses into his Orson Welles voice, I know something's up."

"If I were you, I'd take the train. I noticed lately you get distracted behind the wheel."

"No."

"You mumble. And your eyesight's gotten worse."

"Not really."

"Did I tell you Thane's book is on the short list for a National Book Award?"

"Uh-huh."

"Christ, try and show a little more enthusiasm. I tell you some good news and suddenly you've got that puss on. He's only twenty-four. His first novel. You're so begrudging."

"I complimented him on his book. I just told him I didn't care for the title."

"What's wrong with *The Beveled Heart?*"

"What the hell does it mean? It's pretentious."

"I wouldn't talk about pretention if I was you. All your grim dystopian alleged insights. I'll admit there was a time I found that cynicism tragically romantic, but I've outgrown it."

"Cynicism is realism with a different spelling," Baum muttered with a gram of pleasure over his spontaneous aperçu.

"The press said Thane's potential is unlimited," Connie said, "but then they noticed his potential when he was first published in *Zoetrope* and then that short story about the flamingos was highly praised. And now for his first novel to be such a hit."

"It's not his first. I saw his first and it was not very good. He found out a novel may be ten times longer than one of his short stories but it's not ten times harder—it's a hundred times harder. He was right to pull the plug on it."

"I just think you're jealous."

This was why Baum could not talk to Connie anymore. There was a time they could speak, share feelings, argue, disagree, laugh. But that was then and this was now, and all the nows never seemed to be as nice as all the thens.

It was at a lively New Year's Eve party given years ago by the Sid Greens on Central Park West and Ninety-Second Street. Sid was a reporter who specialized in crime, the more lurid the better. Murder, rape, poisoning, strangulation, beheading; you name it, Sid covered it. He and Baum had been friendly, coming up in the ranks of Manhattan magazines, and it continued to amaze and terrorize Baum, the amount of evil lurking everywhere. On the surface very amiable sorts, usually men but sometimes women, who worked next to you at supermarkets, pet shops, the post office; warm, friendly types who smiled, whistled, made jokes, who might stop to help strangers with street directions or come to the aid of a slip and fall victim; ones you could even invite home for dinner with the wife and kids. Any one of them could turn out to have a basement full of bodies, shot, strangled, God knows what—even cannibalized. Sid wrote colorfully about such people like the police getting a warrant and entering the home of a man who couldn't have been more social and sweet, teaching fifth graders in a public school, only to find reams of porn magazines, shocking videos, pictures of women being tied up, not to mention the knives, a machete, handcuffs, rubber gloves, shoes, underwear and body parts of half a dozen coeds. This too is part of humanity, Baum thought, of God's plan if you believe the clergy. We mortals just don't understand it but have faith, the dismembered co-eds all accrue to something larger and more beautiful. Thane would not touch this subject matter, but Baum would, as Dostoevsky might have, even though the corroded heart of man would not sell thirty-six thousand copies.

But this was no time to pester his friend for the morbid details of the latest treachery that enabled Sid Green to set his table. Everyone was drinking. Drinking and enjoying this New Year's party, unaware that the deadliest killer was loose in the room, hiding in plain sight. It was the clock ticking away lethally toward midnight. Out with the old year, limping its way to the finish line battered and bruised and in with the new year and a hopeful batch of dreams and schemes to beat the house. And there is Baum, standing alone, awash in melancholy and "Auld Lang Syne," unable to help noticing the willowy brunette, the "long goody" as his brother would have referred to her.

"Who is that apparition in black velvet with the nine-year-old date in the Ralph Lauren blazer and slacks?" Baum asked Sid Green. "I'm waiting for the kid to pull out a cigarette case, tap a Marlboro on it and light up."

"C'mon, I'll introduce you."

Connie, in Saint Laurent with every curve of her body coming to a beckoning conclusion, had been invited and taken Thane to the party so he could see the midnight fireworks. Sid Green brought Baum over to Connie and said, "Connie Lister, Asher Baum."

"Oh my goodness," she said, "what a nice surprise. You're the only person in my life I ever wrote a fan letter to, and you were nice enough to answer. Thane, come over here I want you to meet a very brilliant man."

"How do you do?" Baum said, offering his hand.

"How do you do?" Thane said, shaking hands. Thane looked at his mother, saw how she was staring at Baum and gave the stranger the once over. Baum was gobsmacked to learn she was the author of his most enthusiastic fan mail and as the two eased off in a corner by themselves and talked, Thane managed to tilt a full glass of Shirley onto Baum's Saks tweed sport coat. Connie was horrified and it was the one and only time Baum ever heard her speak sternly to her son. After his talking-to, Thane curled up on the floor of the empty study and fell asleep. For Connie and Baum, who talked till dawn, the new year, already rushing forward, did so with all the promise they both had been looking for.

If Baum could not talk to Connie anymore, that certainly wasn't the case when they met. They traded autobiographies; she was the educated looker, raised in the frivolous city of film and television, married to a brilliant doctor who simply had no time for her between patients and his ocular innovations. After him to a famous architect who lost sexual interest in her for whatever utterly incomprehensible reason, and so she fell into an affair with his good friend, yet another creative powerhouse, finally winding up alone and loving it in a pretty part of the Berkshires, where she raised an especially smart son. She had vowed to never marry again but along came Baum. Intellectual, determined to challenge no less than the Russian masters and Kafka, she saw in him the knight she knew didn't exist but longed for.

He captivated her with his own memoir spun out over drinks at Chumley's or the Minetta Tavern or over dim sum in Chinatown and at the galleries downtown he had once loved with Tyler. She spent more time at her Manhattan pied-à-terre, not that she ever adapted to the city, but it was the only way she could spend more time with him. Sometimes he would drive to her country house where she cooked for him. Those dinners included her son, and every once in a while, on a Manhattan date, a Broadway show, the Met, maybe a special meal at Le Cirque, she would ask if he minded if she brought Thane. She said she wanted to introduce him to culture, art, music, plays. He minded a little but not so much that it was a deal breaker. Like with the actor she once dated, who took her to Paris and she brought Thane along, she took him to Venice when Baum brought her there for a week. It had become clear to him that it was a package deal and if you wanted Connie, you bought Connie and Thane. He didn't love it, he didn't hate it, but he loved her and if that was the price for her quirk, he felt she was worth it. If only Thane wasn't such a snotty little know-it-all.

Included in the details of his Brooklyn upbringing and the follies of his failed marriages was Tyler, his second wife whom he spoke of sparingly with some sarcasm, and of course, his lofty goals. Meanwhile, he made his living with articles, some book reviews, even some film criticism now and then for small magazines plus his published nonfiction, particularly his long piece comparing Bruno Bettelheim's take on concentration camp life with Primo Levi's which made some light noise in tiny circles. What his aim was, he poured out to Connie, what he longed for and was certain he could accomplish, was to create from his imagination; to write fiction, not just report news but to fabricate stories that move people, that resonated with their emotions, their most passionate desires and fears. Let lesser minds strike it rich with transient bestsellers. He could not waste his life on such drivel. To sell is to sell out.

Now with Connie behind him he felt more confident than ever. She told him back then in her bedroom as they lay there after having made love, "You will make it because you write fine sentences, and you have a first-class mind. You are not delusional. You see life for what it is, not for how people would like it to be. Your aims are worthy, and I will help support them. I read a few of your short stories and I know what you're going for. I believe in your future."

After this little Knute Rockne moment, it was back for a second round of lovemaking. That was how it was at first but as the years passed the finish line had never been crossed. The novels were turned out laboriously, some plays had "some good things in them" the critics wrote, but Dostoevsky and Kafka had nothing to worry about and Connie's misplaced faith in his gift became an issue.

He was shaping up as a diligent craftsman, turning out inconsistent works that sometimes showed the influence of the greats. As the years bled away, Connie, who was used to geniuses, found herself cheerleading a very decent, loving husband with admirable ambitions who just didn't have the chops. Certainly not the dynamo her first husband had been, or her second. Under the circumstances, is it really so paranoid to suspect your wife of becoming excited by a brother who is everything you're not or a scenic designer she once slept with who is indeed a genius and lives behind the hedges down the road? Add to this the suppressed anger over her obsessive adulation for an arrogant little polymath, his gift now confirmed by what Baum deemed a potpourri of crass philistines. Between him and the little putz (as Baum called him), the putz always came first. This little king, no longer so little but still a king, the king of Thebes if you had a nasty mind, now winds up on the short list for a National Book Award. Is it any wonder I talk to myself? Baum thought. It all seemed to him like yet another injustice in this malicious existence that tries fobbing its malice off as indifference.

What's with Baum?

Thane had a bachelor pad in New York in the East Village. It was a charming old loft that he lived and worked in but he spent weekends at his mother's country house where he loved to hike in the woods, read, swim, build cozy fires in the winter. Often he'd bring up some date for the weekend to exercise his libido and where did he find such sculpted goddesses? Where in the world do these creatures exist? Baum wondered. Models, actresses, ravishing beyond human comprehension. Like they just stepped out of a spaceship from another planet where perfection is the norm. Yes, he's a good-looking kid and now very successful but underneath he's a mama's boy. They'll find out. Now he's apparently in love with one. She doesn't know what she's getting into. Hey, do I care?

"What do you think Scott, my agent, wants to see me about?" Baum queried himself as he drove along the highway into Manhattan the following day.

"I don't know," he replied. At a traffic stop a car pulled abreast of him and could see him talking animatedly to himself. The woman driving it thought nothing of it, shrugged, pulled off.

"He sounded a little serious on the phone," Baum said to Baum.

"Well, you know Scott. He can be a tad dramatic."

"I don't know."

"Or do you know?"

"What are you implying? I wish you wouldn't be so damn coy all the time."

"Think, Asher. Why all of a sudden does he want to speak with you and not on the phone?"

"You're getting me worried."

"I didn't like the sound of it."

"You thinking of that woman?"

"When?"

"Cindy, Mindy Loo. The Chinese one whatever her name was."

"It was Cindy Tanaka and she was Japanese. She interviewed you about your play opening."

"She liked my play."

"Yes. And you thought she was so brilliant."

"She asked all the right questions. She got all the references. She was up on her Hannah Arendt. I was impressed."

"You think she could be causing trouble?"

"What kind of trouble? She interviewed me, we hit it off, clearly liked the play."

"Asher, it's me you're talking to."

"What are you saying?"

"After the interview you were in the elevator alone with her."

"Yeah, so?"

"So did you touch her?"

"Touch her?"

"You heard me. Don't act so innocent. Did you come on with her?"

"I most certainly did not."

"You didn't grab her? Press up against her?"

"Is she saying that?"

"I don't know but Scott sounded concerned. I love that word. Bad but not yet fatal—on the way to fatal."

"At most I may have put my hands on her shoulders and gave her an affectionate compliment. She was a bright charming girl so if I said you're very bright or you have a lovely personality, is that so bad?"

"That's what you said?"

"Or you're the best-looking reporter who ever interviewed me. If I even said that. I don't remember."

"Uh-huh. I'm not buying it."

"For Christ's sake, what is she saying?"

"I don't know."

"I think you know more than you're saying."

Baum rolled on in his Volvo, a car he found charmless but that Connie thought extremely safe and efficient on the country roads. But now he was turning off the George Washington Bridge and heading down the West Side Highway.

When he turned off the drive at Battery Park and hit city traffic his claustrophobia set in. The fear of being trapped and suffocating was a new gift of the gods. It had set in at fifty when he spiraled down in an underground parking garage circling lower and lower and a mysterious panic gripped him. From that moment he added another shock to the thousand natural shocks the flesh is heir to. Claustrophobia—God forbid he should miss a symptom. Congested as he was in bumper-to-bumper stagnation, his heart started pumping harder as he thought about why Scott wanted to see him in person. His mood, which was starting to percolate with anticipatory anxiety, caused him to open the window for air. Maybe it has nothing to do with that crazy Asian woman, he told himself. Who did her something? I told her she was nice looking. *If* I even told her. That makes me some kind of an outlaw?

The traffic took forever to get through and he found himself stuck behind a garbage truck as sanitation workers methodically heaved black polyethylene bags full of the population's detritus into their vehicle while Baum muttered imprecations and his systolic number climbed. When the truck cleared and he could advance, his mind elsewhere, in a vapor lock, he failed to brake in time before bumping gently into the car in front of him. The driver, a nasty-looking piece of work with tattoos and a look on his face like Baum had just murdered his child, gave him a treacherous glare. Stepping out of his car to make sure his precious SUV hadn't suffered a gram of trauma and finding none, he stepped back into his car and gave Baum a middle finger before driving off.

The last thing Baum wanted was to find himself in a road rage drama with a tattooed stranger. In this city any citizen could be an ex-Marine, trained to kill, armed to the teeth and with post-traumatic stress disorder. Connie had wanted to buy a gun years ago but he forbade it. For all her insistence on how safe the country was versus the city, she still wanted to have a weapon. Baum made his case and prevailed. He felt it was folly, there could be an accident and she could shoot someone by mistake. He was sure if that happened it would be him and not Thane that wound up nailed. It was one of the few arguments he had won with her. Of all the ways to die, Baum did not want to die violently. Years ago a man on the Staten Island Ferry had been slaughtered by a crackpot who ran him through with a Samurai sword. Imagine, Baum thought, there are so many ways to go but if someone offered to bet you'd get run through with a Samurai sword on the Staten Island Ferry, you'd be a sucker not to take that bet.

Baum pulled into the closest garage and for a measly eighteen dollars parked his car.

Josh lived in a new, lovely apartment at Battery Park. Much glass all around. Glass, the building material of modern man. If ancient man had glass, the pyramids would have been see-through and you could feast your eyes on mummies in their beautifully painted sarcophagi if that was your thing. Baum always thought the worst job in the world was to be a servant of the Pharaoh because when your master died you got buried along with him even if you were in perfect health. To serve the master in the afterlife was their duty and everybody was happy in this delusion, though Baum wondered if the servants talked in private about handing in their notice.

In Josh's apartment the views were spectacular. From every room you saw the East River, the Hudson, and in the

distance the Statue of Liberty pretending to welcome immi-
grants in search of a better life.

"What can I do for you, Asher? You have another play?"

"Not yet."

"You ever need backing, count me in. I loved your last
one. I couldn't care less what those moron critics said."

"I don't really read reviews."

"Better."

"I only believe the worst about my work and I never trust
the praise."

"Understood. So, better you didn't read anything about
the last one."

"You look good," Baum said. And Josh did. White slacks,
white shirt, tan Gucci loafers, no gray hairs, aging well, a
handsome Italianate face. Somehow, he beat the Jewish
thing. His brother was stylish. He got the few good genes,
Baum thought. All I got was Papa's gallstones and Mama's
depressive worldview.

"So, what do you need?" Josh asked. "And don't be shy.
You know I'd go to the ends of the earth for you. You know
that Asher, right?

Look at this, Asher thought. He's riddled with guilt. All
of a sudden, he can't do enough for me. Since that night.
Since the snowstorm when he knocked off Connie.

Baum sat back on Josh's Danish sofa. All the furniture
was from Denmark except for a couple of Italian chairs which
could have been from the Adirondacks or Jupiter. They were

uncomfortable abstractions that would have made good props for Buster Keaton to try to sit in.

"No play? I hope you're not having one of those bouts of writer's block. What you need is a change of pace. You should come up to Canada with me. Want to go bear hunting? I'm kidding, I'm kidding—you gave me such a look."

"You should be careful, Josh. All that risky stuff. You're not getting any younger. You'll fall off a cliff or ski into a tree." Did they do it in our bed, he wondered, or did Connie at least have the courtesy to do him in the guest room?

"I work out. Did I show you pictures from my trip to Alaska? My life won't be complete till I bag a polar bear. So far no luck."

"And then what do you have, a bearskin rug to make love on?"

"Is that so bad?"

She probably cooked him dinner and of course they had wine. The Clos de Vougeot. Her favorite. It only takes a few glasses to loosen Connie up.

"How's Connie? She in town with you?"

"No, she's up in Connecticut."

I wonder if they planned it or if it was a crime of opportunity.

"You want another Jamaican coffee? Isn't it delicious? Your wife taught me how to make it. You add Tia Maria and whipped cream."

So that's what they were drinking. After the wine and a couple of cups with the Tia Maria for a kicker she'd be ready for anything.

"I've had one and it's already going to my head. I'm not a drinker."

"Go ahead, live. I'm addicted to them."

Baum accepted the second Jamaican coffee. "So if it's not a play you're looking for financing, what? Incidentally, how's your health Asher? You're looking pretty good. I mean you always wear that tragic mask. Last year you gave me quite a scare with all that dizziness business. And they could never find anything. Lucky. You're the one that has to be careful. All those MRIs. Odds are eventually you'll hit a false positive, and they'll have to open you up to check you out."

"I wanted to talk to you about Papa."

"Papa's dead."

"I know he's dead, Josh. What am I, an idiot?"

"You miss him?"

"Don't you?"

"A lot."

"He thought the world of you."

"And you, Asher. They were both very loving parents. Nuts in their ways but pretty terrific. What about Papa?"

"We have to dig him up."

"Pardon me. I don't think I heard you correctly."

"He's been appearing in my dreams lately Josh, and we have to dig him up."

"What are you talking about? Are you crazy?"

"Papa was a Mason."

"Believe me Asher, I know he was a Mason. With the All-Seeing Eye and the handshake. Remember three-five-seven or whatever the hell it was." Baum was starting to feel the effects of the second Jamaican coffee.

"Listen to me, Josh. We were so busy with everything, the funeral, my play, my colonoscopy, you just got back from Africa."

"Get to the point."

"We forgot to bury him in his lambskin apron."

"What lambskin apron?" Josh said. "What the hell are you talking about?"

"It's a Mason thing. You remember he always said, when I die make sure you bury me in my lambskin apron?"

"What have you been smoking, Asher? You want to dig up Papa so we can dress him in that *schmatte*?"

"I have it. It was in that valise. The brown one with his initials. It's important to him."

"He's dead."

"Stop telling me he's dead. I know he's dead. It's a sacred Mason thing. To be buried in the lambskin apron."

"You better get a grip on yourself, kid. Okay, we blew it. It's a shame but what's done is done."

"It was important to him, his last request."

"I got it. We made a mistake but he's never going to know, Asher."

33

"It's for eternity, Josh. He wanted to be buried for eternity in his lambskin apron."

"When he was alive, Asher. He wanted that when he was alive. We screwed up but it's silly to exhume someone just to dress a dead body in a lambskin apron."

"Silly to you."

"I'm surprised at you. You don't believe in any of that stuff. No religion, no afterlife. To you it's all bullshit. None of it has any meaning. Isn't that one of your big themes?"

"It had meaning to him."

"He's dead."

"Will you stop telling me he's dead? For Christ's sake, what is the big deal here?"

"I don't believe this. You, who calls the whole universe a cosmic booby hatch, much ado about nothing, absurd."

"It's all of those things but it was a request from our father."

"Asher, you can't just dig somebody up. You need a funeral director, there's lots of paperwork. I read about it once in an article. Unless they changed the law you need a good reason before you can get a permit to do this."

"We have a good reason to dig him up."

"What? Because we want to dress him in a lambskin apron?"

"For a Mason it's his last request. They won't deny it. I think the family has to agree."

"I can't agree. The whole thing is too ridiculous. For Christ's sake, let the man rest in peace."

"He's not in peace. And I keep dreaming we failed him."

"It's insane. I'm not letting you dig up poor Papa and change his outfit. This is not a fashion show. It's blasphemy. I don't know what the hell it is."

"I don't like that tone of voice, Josh. We're just having a discussion."

Baum was taking on a slightly pugnacious edge from the modest touch of booze in the coffee cup.

"I'm not discussing this any further. It's too crackpot," Josh said. "Be sensible. For an avowed atheist you're suddenly worried about eternity, the afterlife? Gimme a break."

"Agnostic. Not atheist," Baum said with the barest tinge of slurring.

"Agnostic, atheist. Meanwhile, I'm the more observant Jew and you who don't have a religious bone in your body, who always found the Masons a silly cult with the secret mystic rites, and now you want to desecrate poor Jacob Baum's grave after he's been laid to rest for years so you can make up for the careless mistake you made forgetting to dress him in his lambskin apron. I loved Papa, as I know you did, but forget it. I never heard of such stupidity."

The brothers quarreled and the issue took on greater heat. Hurtful remarks flew back and forth, and as Baum was becoming more uninhibited from the Tia Maria, he said,

"Don't think you're pulling the wool over my eyes. I wasn't born yesterday."

"I don't know what the hell you're talking about," Josh said.

"I'll bet you don't," Asher said and stormed out having failed to secure a commitment regarding the exhumation of Jacob Israel Baum and his lambskin apron.

He sat for a while on a bench staring at the Statue of Liberty as he let the fresh air revive his sobriety. Josh left the building, saw him sitting there, ignored him and drove off in an Uber.

"Did you see how he squirmed when I called him on Connie?"

"You didn't call him. You only said he wasn't pulling the wool over your eyes and that you weren't born yesterday. Two clichés."

"He knows what I meant. It brought him up short."

"I didn't think so. You're barking up the wrong tree. He may never have touched her."

"Now who's talking in clichés."

A woman walking by saw him talking to himself and detoured well around his bench, speeding up her pace.

"And what was all that talk about digging up Papa? You, who are certain when it's over you don't exist anymore."

"You're taking his side? I promised Papa and then I forgot."

"How could you forget such a meaningful oath?"

"My play was failing in rehearsal, then the heart attack—"

"You didn't have a heart attack."

"A kidney stone can mimic a heart attack."

"You didn't have a kidney stone."

"Arthritis can mimic a stone and I have arthritis. Christ, with all that mimicking going on I forgot. Okay? People forget. Then Papa appeared in my dreams and wept over his Masonic apron and I woke up sweating with guilt. Josh doesn't get it. He's never had a guilty moment in his life."

Baum thought about how different they were. Same parents, same gene pool, same upbringing, and yet so different. He sat on the bench thinking about the old man. He thought of the even older man, not his father Jacob, but his grandfather whom he never met, Samuel.

Samuel was an actor in the theater in Berlin. He had a large following, and amongst his admirers was Joseph Goebbels, who attended plays often. One night after a show in which Samuel Baum appeared, *Der goldene Pierrot*, an operetta, Goebbels came backstage to hit on one of the pretty ingenues. While waiting for her to get out of her costume and change into her street clothes, he ran into Samuel Baum and the two men got to talking. Goebbels had nothing but praise for the actor. He told Baum that he had enjoyed him many times and then asked politely if he might offer him a bit of advice. Samuel Baum, curious, said of course, whereupon Goebbels said, "If I were you, I would take my wife and leave Germany right away."

The actor asked why. Samuel Baum was fully aware of the steady erosion of civil liberties for the Jews but assumed optimistically that persecution had reached a high point from which it would de-escalate, and Germany would gradually be returning to normal. "Because," Goebbels said, "in the coming year, things are going to get very bad for the Jews— 1937 was not good but 1938 is going to be much worse. I warn you because you are an artist and I respect your work. You should leave now while you have a chance."

Goebbels' advice sank in. Baum took his wife and with the help of a few distant relatives, fled to London. There they stayed for a few years, and when the bombs came to England, they managed to get to America, settling in New York in a dreary flat on Eldridge Street. This was not the kind of living Samuel Baum was used to, and from the very beginning he hated America. He could never adjust, always grumpy, always critical, bitter, and missing his native city terribly. Limited by his English and forced to work in a restaurant, he decided to lay his head down on the subway tracks in front of an oncoming train, which for Sam Baum wrote *das Ende* to Roosevelt, Joe DiMaggio, and Frank Sinatra. He died on April 20, Hitler's birthday, merely a coincidence said his only child, Jacob, who had no patience for anything mystical or to do with fate. Shortly after that Jacob moved his wife and sons to Prospect Park, near the Brooklyn Museum and Brooklyn Public Library.

Jacob was, like Samuel, an intellectual, a graduate of City College, a professor of languages at a private high school, carrying Samuel's gene for misanthropy and discontent. The world was a cruel, unfathomable place, he felt, made worse, not better by the people in it. How could he not be disillusioned? He was raised to adore and pray for deliverance to a divinity who would not return a phone call. Everywhere Jacob looked for an answer he got nothing. Spinoza, a landsman, failed him with his foolish pantheism. It was no help that God dwells in us all, in every stone and flower. Jacob was looking for a God who, contrary to Spinoza's, stood apart from existence, viewed it from above and was willing to throw in an occasional miracle if needed. Nor could Jacob make the Kierkegaardian leap of faith. Faith was fine he felt, but a little proof never hurts a dicey leap. He toyed with the Eastern religions but could not renounce a single desire and when last seen here on earth, he was a practicing Mason, into all the secret mumbo jumbo. Even then, he was selective, enjoying the philanthropy, shaking hands ritualistically and hoping for the best, and then his heart stopped and if there was anything more, he was now finding it out.

As for his wife, Rachel, she was a pill with a dark vision of life and people, and much as Baum wanted to prove her wrong, it was hard. Rachel was cultivated, and she bore her husband two sons. First Asher, then Joshua. Asher inherited his grandfather's DNA for histrionic suffering and his father's love of literature. At ten his mother bought him a microscope because he showed curiosity about science. When she took a safety pin and pricked her finger to get some blood so he could examine it on a slide, he fainted.

When the microscope failed to reveal the secrets of the universe, he switched to a telescope, and while scanning the heavens required no bloodletting, the night sky made his adrenaline spurt with terror. Like his father, he sought always for answers; answers for something, for anything, for everything. Meanwhile his parents took him to plays and films, concerts and art galleries. His mother encouraged him to practice his flute so he could play Mozart and sampled marijuana with him. When he wrote an article at seventeen on Faust, he got it published in the July issue of a small magazine.

Brother Josh was another story entirely. Also quite intelligent, Josh had no patience with literature. Words on paper bored him, and he dropped out of NYU in his sophomore year to enlist in the Marines. He was shipped to Iraq during the war, where he made the kind of actual existential choices his brother only read about. He risked death; he caused death. He executed a young Arab with his own pistol for trying to sabotage a truck with medical supplies. He took chances, and the idea of eternal extinction didn't seem to faze him. Dying in combat was an acceptable option. It was not so much bravery as the implications of oblivion didn't seem to sink in or if they did they were not as unpleasant to him as to his older brother. To walk amongst the lifeless bodies of his closest buddies in the desert was to him the business of war. His pals were dead, gone, got it, let's move on. To Asher even the passing of a hearse in Brooklyn weakened his knees.

Josh got out of the Marines, was shipped back to the West Coast and spent two weeks in Las Vegas with some guys he had served with overseas before returning to New York. In Vegas he gambled and won a great deal of money. Good luck followed him everywhere from the slots to the crap tables and the wheel, and he did so well at the black-jack table, a game he had never played before, the pit bosses thought he might be counting cards. Back in Manhattan he used the winnings to invest on the say-so of a friend in a small real estate enterprise which turned into a bonanza and by thirty money was no longer an issue in his life. He had all he needed to travel, hunt, climb and charm the ladies. He and Asher loved one another technically but Josh never quite "got" his brother who always seemed like a lost poet with pipe dreams and a siege mentality. He didn't understand why Asher always seemed so scared of life when it was there for the taking. Josh never married, preferring the adventure each new conquest brought.

Asher, born into loneliness the way one is born into autism, proposed at twenty-one to a lovely girl fresh out of Barnard. Her name was Nina Glass and she lived on Central Park West. They met auspiciously for two young intellectuals seeking wisdom. It was an unfurnished hall on the Lower East Side. In this no-frills room in a dilapidated townhouse a charmless little man was giving a lecture on Aesthetic Realism. Baum found it hard to buy into the philosophy of the oneness of opposites and as far as aesthetics went, he had read Kant on the subject and found it hard to understand. He concluded that aesthetics was not a mode of thought that did anything for the things that haunted him, though like his father he was ready to look anywhere for a remedy. But in that run-down little lecture hall where he did not find the answers he was seeking, he did find a pretty Jewish brunette named Nina Glass.

Both had come alone and after the lecture somehow found themselves mumbling together about the content of the talk. After a few minutes of chatting he suggested a cappuccino and she bit. Over a table lit only by a candle, their chat began with Eli Siegel, the founder of Aesthetic Realism and segued into Plato's concept of the beautiful, on to Oscar Wilde on beauty, Dorian Gray into the Irish writers to the Russian writers, then to European literature, foreign cinema, the French *nouvelle vague*, Ingmar Bergman's films and a check please followed by a cab ride to her place, her parents being away in London and so, jackpot. The three months that followed were a delight for both of them. Getting to know one another, walks in the park, the Angelika, her parents' home in the Hamptons and stolen moments of sex as they both still lived at home. Oh, and she had a twin sister at UCLA, her name was Ann. Nina worked at the reception desk in an art gallery. He worked as a guard at a museum on the Upper East Side. It was a dull job sitting alone all night hoping no one would try and run off with a Kandinsky but it had the advantage of giving him lots of reading time.

And did there come a time, as lawyers ask, when they married? There did. Ann came east from college to attend the wedding and he set eyes on Nina's double. He was struck not only by how identical they looked but how their manner coincided. A few months later when she finished school and moved back to New York and Baum and Nina saw her socially quite often and she came to a dinner regularly at their apartment on Cornelia Street, some strange magic occurred. It happened one night when Baum was dining with both sisters and couldn't help marveling at how alike they actually were, even to the way they dressed in skirts and sweaters and both chose earth tones. And for whatever reason as he sat in the living room with them and gazed, the clear, vivid and overwhelming thought entered his mind, as eureka as energy equals mass times the speed of light squared hit Einstein, that he loved Ann, not Nina. Thus began a month's long affair that started weeks later after agonizing and totally bewildering thoughts with believe it or not, a kiss in the dark. The three of them were watching a movie on TV at Baum and Nina's apartment. Nina left the room to open a bottle of wine when Baum leaned forward at the precise moment Montgomery Clift kissed Elizabeth Taylor in extreme closeup and kissed Ann. He instantly knew that she was up for it by the way she responded, meeting him halfway. The rest, as they say, is history.

The puzzling thing was not so much why he might be attracted to a carbon copy of his wife but why his love and attraction for Nina were fading, given that on paper she offered him the precise rewards as Ann. Both were easy laughers, bright, fans of the same books and plays, music and films, both equally adventurous in bed.

He was familiar with Nietzsche's thoughts on the matter: That no two things are truly identical if you look closely enough. But close as he looked, the differences were negligible, not enough to prize one over the other. And yet he did. Nina excited him less and less. He was tormented by the craziness of it all and unwilling to continue the affair on moral grounds, confessed to Nina who left him that day. Soon after, the intensity of his romantic liaison with Ann sputtered and they agreed to part. His conclusion was that there was a mystery to love, to romantic attraction, that he would never fathom, and it became the second-most important puzzle he wanted an answer to. Second only to why is there something rather than nothing?

Asher popped for the garage usury and lit out for his five thirty sit-down with book agent Scott Bell.

The two men had worked together for the last five years after Asher and his former agent, Bob Bluestone, split acrimoniously over a series of unreturned phone calls and a quip Bluestone was alleged to have made at a cocktail party about Baum's latest book and a paper shredder. Faced with the sclerotic congestion, potholes, broken lights and Con Ed construction versus the FDR Drive, Baum chose the streets. The Drive, if clear, would have gotten him there in half the time but god forbid for some reason the lanes weren't moving; the thought of being stuck, frozen in traffic on the highway, with his luck seemed inevitable. In the streets, he could zig and zag his way to freedom.

As it turned out the traffic was moderate, and he enjoyed looking out the window at a town that still held him in its charismatic grip. True, it had changed enormously since he always pictured it scored by Rogers and Hart. According to the news, this great town was currently at war with rats and had appointed a Rat Czar. Asher imagined a scenario where the rats, through their numbers and cleverness, had taken over Manhattan, bound and gagged the Rat Czar and ran everything. Rats took over the restaurants, the supermarkets, the high-end jewelry and clothing stores. They ran Tiffany's and Bergdorf's and dominated Broadway, producing all the shows. Baum guessed rats would be sharp enough to figure a way to reduce ticket costs.

By now he had found a station on the car radio that played oldies but goodies and he listened to Cole Porter, George Gershwin and Irving Berlin. Baum wished he could have lived in the twenties and thirties when Manhattan actually had the glamour that Hollywood celebrated in so many movies. In his rosy-colored daydreams he lived in a

Manhattan where men came home from work and changed into tuxedoes and their beautiful wives into expensive gowns. They welcomed a few similarly attired friends over for cocktails and smart conversation and if they went out it was to Twenty-One, El Morocco or an opening night at the Booth or the Morosco and not into the pitch black of country roads where you could easily hit a deer. Did such a New York ever really exist or only via MGM?

Asher brought himself back from his Golden Age fantasies just as he was cruising through Irving Place and heading around Gramercy Park. He had always wanted to live on Gramercy Park but had never pulled it off. When he finally did move out of his parents' home and into the city it was to a small apartment below street level in the Village. "I live under Bedford Street," he told people, and the entrance was four steps down so it was true. Asher experienced a wave of anger over spending less and less time in the city as the years passed. He kicked himself for being a victim of Connie's gracious manipulation. As he bounced along over assorted potholes what popped into his head was a long-gone coffee shop where he lived when he first moved to the Village. He and his pals used to sit over endless cappuccinos and discuss life, the arts, women, the joys and ruthlessness of everything. He didn't keep up with any of those friends anymore, those wonderful, colorful wannabes. Everyone moved on with their lives for better or worse.

What's with Baum?

Peter Yellin came to mind as Asher drove daydreaming. Yellin was a writer friend when they were both in their twenties. Both aspired to outdo O'Neill and Dostoevsky. Anything less was a sellout, unworthy of time spent at the Olivetti portable. Yellin also lived downtown, and they hung out together at Raoul's and the many little cafes that flickered briefly and then went out one by one like lights on the Christmas tree. Intellectual products of the City College cafeteria, he and Yellin were a grand duo. Yellin loved *The Iceman Cometh* and *Long Day's Journey Into Night*. He wrote rapidly and with intensity the way it's alleged Van Gogh painted. He turned out one-acters and larger plays and sometimes short stories. Nothing ever happened with most of them. The plays were practically all unproduced; the stories rarely saw print. When, after a few years of disciplined writing Yellin managed to get a play on off-Broadway, everything went wrong. The cast did not get along; the director treated it as a realistic melodrama when in fact it was a poetic piece. Being foreign, the director never understood where the emphasis on each line should fall. The costumes were lackluster, the set understated. It was perpetual agony for Yellin, who complained to Baum and brought him down to view a run-through. Baum thought it an unmitigated catastrophe and advised his friend to fold it rather than absorb a critical bloodbath.

By then, Yellin was sleeping with the leading lady who took direction from him rather than the director causing further chaos. The affair between author and star resulted only in gonorrhea for Yellin and as Baum predicted, the play closed the weekend after it opened. Baum referred to the closing as a mercy killing. Yellin shied away from the theater, never got a novel published and eventually took a job with a public relations firm trying to get their clients' names in tabloid gossip columns. Sometimes it fell to Yellin to keep their names out of the papers, as in driving while intoxicated and running over a pedestrian or caught shoplifting. Needless to say, Yellin did not pose a threat to the author of *Long Day's Journey* and wound up living in Santa Barbara.

Baum in contrast was adamant about not selling out and supported himself freelancing and tutoring. His attempts at fiction showed promise but were never as good as his magazine articles on the world events or cultural issues which sold enough for him to survive in Manhattan.

His erudite style was straightforward, perhaps a tad ponderous at times. The word "ponderous" would haunt him through the years. He would more easily make people think than feel and appeared to be more suited to journalism, but he comforted himself with the fact that any number of great writers began as newspapermen. He had trouble creating characters who too often were merely vehicles for his ideas. I know this man, he wanted the reader to feel about his characters. He is me. He shares my longing, my fears. Having read the book and lived through the valleys and peaks of this man's experiences I now see life differently. I don't need God to find meaning. It may be all for nothing but I still say yes to being. That's what Baum wanted the reader to feel closing the covers of his fiction. The problem was he couldn't sell all that because he didn't really buy it himself.

Another friend of those years was Sam Jablon; chubby, likable with a good sense of humor. Here in New York Jablon couldn't get off the schneid. He hung around the theater cafes for hours and dreamed with Baum and kept him laughing and hopeful in moments of doom and gloom. Jablon loved life, loved show business, loved Raoul's cheeseburgers. He also loved women and no amount of rejection or adverse criticism for his satirical output, which was broad and crude, could get him down. No failed script, no brutal shellacking by press when he did get a piece staged or published in an obscure magazine, troubled the captain's mind. Jablon was thought to be by ones more cruel than Baum a rotund boob too silly to take seriously, good for a laugh at his own expense. Meanwhile, Jablon eked out a living selling routines to night club comedians, some bits scoring but most dropping dead, causing the performers to threaten lawsuits and even violence.

Baum thought Jablon was funny without intending to be. Example. It's told that Jablon once found a wallet on Lexington Avenue with a credit card in it, and rather than do the honest thing he tried using the card to buy himself a portable TV set. After he gave the clerk at Bloomingdale's the card to pay, he noticed several of the workers staring and whispering. Moments later two security guards escorted him to an office at the store, and he was arrested. The man who lost the credit card had been Gregory Peck.

True or not, that does encapsulate Jablon. Unable to survive in New York, Jablon moved to Los Angeles where a few of his scripts were turned into situation comedies and were immediately big successes. A hit show opened the door to producing and then to spin-offs of his original show which made him a multimillionaire and earned him the reputation of a genius. Around Hollywood, Jablon's counsel and wisdom were much sought after. Baum had lost touch with Jablon but thought of him with nostalgic fondness. We all had our dreams and ambitions and eventually realized that what Dostoevsky and O'Neill did was harder than we imagined.

Baum pulled up in front of his agent's office building and unwilling to spend another eighteen dollars for an hour's worth of parking, searched high and low for half an hour before filching an open spot within commuting distance of Scott Bell's office.

"I'm glad you could get here," Bell said, adjusting himself behind his desk in a way that reminded Baum of when he was called before his college teacher who read him the riot act for his paper defending Alger Hiss. "Did you hit much traffic driving in?"

Baum recognized this question as a stall. It could be of no possible interest or meaning to Bell whether Baum hit traffic or made the trip in record time. Bell never used the

Drive, living as he did on Sutton Place. Clearly, he was having trouble bringing up an awkward subject.

"The magazine article with your interview—we have an advance copy. I mean it will be out in a week or so."

"Yes? I'm anxious to read it."

"Don't be, Asher. It's not supportive."

The phrase "not supportive" failed to convey the piece's lethal tone but Bell was fussing diplomatically to try and navigate the semantic shoals of what was basically a hatchet job.

"You may want to call your lawyer. I'm no maven on libel. I asked Barry Kirchner in legal to take a look at it. He gave it a quick MRI and didn't think you had a case. Still—"

"My god, what the hell did she say? Can I see it? You have a copy?"

Bell rose and began to search for it amidst the manuscripts and magazines that lay around the office.

"She said you came on with her at the interview and she was taken aback."

"I came on with her?"

"And you grabbed her and tried to kiss her."

"What?" A vein Baum's body seldom used began rising in his neck.

"You fondled her breast?"

"I don't believe she said that."

"Did you touch her?"

"I gave her an antiseptic show business peck on the cheek at the end."

"Apparently she was all shaken up."

"This woman is crazy," Baum yelped, his voice edging upward toward the soprano range.

"She went back and read things you had previously written, and she found clues," Bell said.

"Clues? To what?"

"What she says in the article. Where you give yourself away as a misogynist and a predator."

"I didn't grab her, Scott. Okay, wait—here's what I did. She was so bright, so charming and so complimentary about my writing that when she was leaving, I put one hand on each of her shoulders, made sure I had her full attention and told her what a delight it was to be interviewed by such a perceptive critic and that usually someone as young as she doesn't ask such stimulating questions. I said goodbye and gave her a peck on the cheek. Okay, so maybe I used a scintilla more verve but Christ, I didn't stick my tongue in her ear."

"She doesn't say you stuck your tongue in her ear."

"Why would I stick my tongue in her ear?"

"Calm down, Asher. And you didn't say anything about her eyes? That she had beautiful green eyes?"

"She had green eyes. She had two green eyes. What is this?" Baum was losing patience.

"And you told her green eyes denote passion."

"They do. Look it up. You know who had green eyes? Jane Eyre. You must've read *Jane Eyre*. Christ, what that girl went through."

"And then you kissed her."

"Why would I do something like that? I'd have to be insane."

"And she pushed you off and you fell, the article says."

"She got so nervous. I was pecking her goodbye."

"And you fell and grabbed her breast."

"I was falling. I reached for the first thing handy to break my fall. It happened to be her breast. But it was an accident."

"Look Asher, you don't have to sell me. Sit down. I think you're a little frazzled now."

"I'm a married man. You met Connie. With a wife that looks like Connie you think I'm looking to play around?"

"The problem is Landau."

"Don't tell me."

"You know Landau. And he's already getting pressure from his staff."

Jack Landau, the head of Rhinegold Publishing, had never liked Baum. He never really saw the potential certain ones seem to find in his writing and tepidly agreed to publish him on Scott Bell's urging. Landau found Baum's obsession with the "big questions" tiresome and sophomoric.

"Nobody cares about dark matter. It doesn't impact their daily lives," he told Baum. "Can't you get off that kick and come up with a book that has a little schmaltz? People don't read anymore and certainly not fiction. If they do buy a novel they want a little respite from life's twenty-four seven horror show. For Christ's sake, give 'em some flesh-and-blood human beings and some conflict, a little suspense. You ask why you don't sell."

It was true that Baum's last book did nothing to abuse Landau of the conviction Rhinegold was wasting time trying to push an author whom the critics called preachy. Now, after passing around the advanced copy of this reporter's accusations against Baum, Landau's underlings, all young, many women but even the men, had banded together and suggested the front office honchos should part company with a writer whose behavior did nothing to enhance Rhinegold's reputation.

"Are you going to tell me Landau takes his marching orders from his staff?" Baum said.

"I've made some calls to a few publishers."

"And?" Baum said, his face never more grim.

"You have to understand, publishing is going through a tough time. Landau's right. Nobody reads. And it's not like you were ever a mainstream player."

"So you're telling me Rhinegold's dropping me?"

"People run scared."

"This magazine comes out when?"

"In the next week or two."

"And she accuses me of being a predator?"

"That's the gist of the piece. How she starts off admiring you and your work and winds up bringing a suit against you."

"A suit? For what?"

"The tabloids will probably scream rape."

"Rape? She says I tried to rape her?"

"No, I'm saying the tabloids will probably pick up the story and run with it."

"You buy all this?"

"I definitely don't Asher, but what the hell does it matter what I think? In today's culture an accusal is as good as a conviction."

By now the first beads of sweat began to glisten on Baum's brow.

"Let me ask you, Asher, how will your wife take this?"

"She knows I'd never hit on another woman. We've talked about how out of proportion these things can become."

"Yeah," Bell said, "fidelity is the only answer. I have another client—I won't mention names, an editor. He and his wife are into polyamory. They each go to bed with whomever they want. They've been doing it now for a year and so far it's working but who knows. Talk to me after more time. For a while this whole thing will be white hot. Keep working on your next play or novel. When things calm down, I'll sit with Landau. I have some pull with him. I think Rhinegold is still your best bet if they'll have you."

"I'll sue this woman for defamation."

"You can. It's an uphill fight but who knows. Meanwhile if you need anything, call. You have my cell."

Cut to Baum wandering out of the building in a stupor heading toward his car. By now people were knocking off work and the streets were filling up. He was certain everyone walking to the subways and buses or hailing taxis had received advance copies of the article accusing him of a shameful assault on an innocent young minority girl. He found his car but before going home needed to share his misery and maybe even have a whiskey. He phoned his old comrade in ideas, Amnon Weinstock. He said he was in Manhattan and could he come by to say hello. Weinstock was surprised and happy to hear from him.

"I'll put up the tea kettle," he said.

Friends from high school, they saw each other rarely now but checked in by phone intermittently to gossip and celebrate a new book or disembowel some pseudo-intellectual writer or politician. Weinstock looked rabbinical with his beard and yarmulke.

The two had met playing basketball against one another at sixteen. Baum was an acceptable schoolyard athlete and Weinstock was a dominant center for the Yeshiva team. After a game the two got to chatting, discovered they both liked Kafka, Auden and the New York Knickerbockers. Baum found basketball fun to watch but argued with his new friend who would get very excited in the final minutes with the game on the line. Baum's position was that it was not worth the intensity Weinstock was investing in the final score. Who won or lost meant nothing in the larger or smaller scheme of things. Weinstock argued that the outcome of the game meant exactly as much as the entire universe does—no more, no less.

What's with Baum?

The insight, depressing as it was, fell on fertile soil. The two were always arguing, debating; the disputations Weinstock called their conflicting viewpoints in his Talmudic style. He had gone on to become a great scholar, a professor, a lecturer, a writer on esoteric subjects for prestigious journals. He philosophized on everything from the writing of Husserl and Wittgenstein to the perversion of the dialectic in Eastern European politics, his predictions being prescient. Their lives diverged when Weinstock went abroad to teach in England and then Israel. He wrote profound articles on Arab-Israeli conflicts, the endless suffering and seemingly unsolvable problems of the Middle East for which he offered humane and sensible solutions, provocative and inspiring. Years later he came back to teach and lecture at several Ivy League schools. To Baum, he was always a good friend and the two touched base in person every year to continue their disputations over blintzes at an Upper West Side dairy restaurant. Baum couldn't believe his good luck finding a parking space right in front of the old building on Riverside Drive in which Weinstock was a tenant along with an economist and a renowned violin player. It was like hitting the lottery, he thought.

Weinstock was delighted by the unexpected visit from his old friend and they hugged hello. It had been a while since Baum had seen Weinstock, and the man's crown baldness had evolved dramatically, though well hidden by his ever-present skullcap.

"So good to see you, Asher. A very serendipitous plea-sure. You look well."

"You look well too," Asher said.

"I'm tip-top. Did you by chance read Rapkin's piece on Putin and Russian Paranoia? I thought it was brilliant."

"I clipped it out but never got back to it. I have it."

"You sounded a little *shvach* on the phone. Everything all right?"

Baum explained the situation. A crazy woman was over-reacting to the most innocent gesture and what should have been taken as a compliment turned into a whole *tzimmes* of harassment or worse. All this would probably find its way to the tabloids and had already cost him his publisher who wanted no part of any scandal.

"They dropped me. And you know what craven sheep people are. I already sense from my agent's euphemisms I'm en route to pariahville. And Connie. Not that she'd believe any of this but the way things have been going between us these days, she'll believe it."

"Trouble at home?"

"I don't know. Somewhere along the line we got untracked."

"Meanwhile your stepson has got quite a success on his hands. And his first novel. Such a future. That should give you some *nachas*."

"You read the book?"

"I bought it. I haven't gotten to it yet. I'll let you know."

"I can't stand the little *momzer*. You're the only one I can talk to. I can't talk to anybody anymore. Only myself."

"That's a bad sign, Asher."

"He's a pampered little arrogant prince. She always fell all over him like he was the second coming of the Messiah."

Weinstock lent a sympathetic ear, part rabbi, part shrink, part good friend. He assured Baum the move was not to panic.

"We live in an awkward time. Extremists, one of our two major parties festering away, anti-Semitism, low pop culture. But fear not, Asher, the human body has a tendency to heal itself. All this will not last and rationality will return."

"I agree, it's transient," Asher said. "But till it's over along the way there will be blood, lives ruined."

"Yes, but there will also be heroes. Think how once the ones blacklisted by McCarthy suffered and yet with time, McCarthy became a symbol of disgrace and those persecuted are now thought of as noble."

"She says I kissed her—"

"I quote Martin about the moral arc of the universe being long but bending toward justice."

"Yes, Amnon, but before that arc bends it could easily break."

"I know it's awful to suffer a slander or a libel but sometimes it's best to bide your time and do nothing rather than take arms against a sea of troubles and by opposing make them a lot worse."

"You studied law. Can't I sue for defamation of character?"

Weinstock now at his most Talmudic responded, "Think, Asher. You possess a certain character. You're a man of many parts, many ideas, feelings, emotions. You're a husband, an artist, a citizen, a philosopher. So you sue, get into a dogfight, pay extortionate fees to lawyers, make headlines in the yellow press; be reviled, parodied on social media. You could be right and still lose your case. And of course, there's the court of public opinion. Sometimes we have to suffer in silence till the arc bends our way. But Asher, you know all this."

Baum sipped the tea and digested Weinstock's wisdom. He sighed with resignation.

"And what's all this?" he finally asked, surveying the clothes and valises, some already packed, the pictures taken down, *tchotchkes* bubble wrapped. "What's going on? Are you moving? Have you taken a position abroad? Oxford? The Sorbonne?"

"Not exactly, good friend," Weinstock said. "You're right about one thing. I'm moving."

"Where? What goes?"

"To New Orleans."

"Tulane?"

"No, I've decided I've had enough. I'm packing it in."

"No—"

"Yes, I've always been a great music lover. Well, we've listened to the Beethoven quartets together and the Schubert and Bartok. I know how much you love the second movement of the Sibelius violin piece. And if you recall I always had an interest in gospel and jazz. I wrote about the musical structure of the blues. I don't know if you read it but I had quite a long piece on the origins of Delta songs and hymns for *Tikkun*, a Jewish journal. I'm sure you know it all originated in the slavery period. Anyway, I have some friends down there who have a jazz band. They play mostly traditional tunes, ragtime, church music, music of the parades and whorehouses. Anyway they've invited me to join them."

"Join them? A band? What do you mean?"

"Every once in a while I sit in with them and I always have the time of my life."

"But you don't play an instrument. You gave up the violin years ago."

"Yes, but I'm good at keeping time and those authentic bands often had a tambourine player. Christ, Asher, I can bang a tambourine."

"Yes but—"

"I've gotten so fed up with the world and thought to myself, Wouldn't that be a blast spending time doing tambourine in the Crescent City? It's such a lovely town, so charming with the architecture, the garden district, Lake Pontchartrain and Asher, the food. Those beignets and the blackened red fish. No more sweating over articles, defending political positions, explicating texts for college kids who go on to run corporations or work in advertising agencies. There's nothing wrong with it but I've been at it for years and I'm bored. I've had it with the academic world, the life of the mind. Keeping time with a hot band is pure pleasure. You hear what I'm saying?"

Baum heard but he could not process the information. He sat open-mouthed. The thought of Amnon Weinstock in his yarmulke sitting in on tambourine was like stepping into a Magritte. Okay, so he wanted to retire; a bit young but still, let him travel, write his memoirs, take up painting, but keeping time in a smoke-filled bar on Bourbon Street? Give me a break. And yet here he was, not a whit less sharp than when he parsed Hegel so brilliantly. It was as if a doctor had given him a few months to live and he had decided to run amuck fulfilling his bucket list. But he was not moribund, not confused, lucid as a diamond.

"You should see, Asher, I'm like a new person. It brings out the wild man in me. I wear my embroidered yarmulke. It's a little more theatrical. You think I'm silly?"

Dazed, Baum wished him luck, they hugged, Weinstock said if Baum was ever down South to be sure to come by and listen. The band was called The White Chocolate Dandies. In the twenties, Weinstock explained, a band of African American musicians had been called The Chocolate Dandies and since all the newcomers in his band were Caucasian, they named themselves in homage.

I get it, thought Baum, it's clever, it's well intended but I'd pick something blander. Just to keep your house from being burned down. Moments later Baum was pulling out of his parking space and curving on to the highway. By the time he was clear of the tollbooth he was already in deep conversation.

"Can you believe Weinstock? Abandoning his intellectual life to whack a tambourine?"

"If you remember he had an eclectic record collection. Not just longhair. His palate was always wide."

"I remember when we were young he played a little trumpet. He played Bach. Then he switched to violin. But who knew he'd end up like this. He's a deep thinker. I don't get it."

"We've discussed this before. You can't compare cerebral pleasures to the call of the primitive; the enjoyment of music trumps all other pleasures. Especially music with a beat."

"I—I—but—"

"Never underestimate the sheer joy of melody and rhythm."

"I suppose—"

"Meanwhile, my friend, you stand to be the subject of some nasty allegations."

"Does it make sense to you? I'm going to hit on a total stranger who's interviewing me? What am I? Suicidal?"

"If you didn't do it you have nothing to worry about."

"You don't believe me?"

"I'm just saying—"

"What? What are you saying?"

"I'm saying you're playing around with the truth, no?"

"What?" Asher said innocently. "You think I made a move on her?"

"To thine own self be true. Shakespeare knew what he was talking about. To thine own self. Not always so easy."

"You're telling me you believe I got fresh with that girl. Cindy, Lindy."

"Cindy Tanaka. I think you've been going through a bad emotional period for a while now."

"So what? Okay—yes, you're saying I tried to kiss her? I kissed her?"

"Level with me, Asher. I'm not going to tell anybody."

"I'm coming undone. Everything has been piling up on me over the last year—or should I say years—I'm not responsible if I lose control sometimes. I used to count on Connie. We don't kiss anymore. I wanted to kiss somebody. Is that so terrible?"

"I don't think Connie will see it your way."

"Don't say that. I still have feelings for Connie. Or have I just grown so dependent on her?"

"She thought she was marrying Philip Roth or Saul Bellow."

"I have not lived up to my potential."

"True. And now Thane is living up to your potential."

"And don't think she doesn't have her own problems. I should have seen right from the start her relationship to Thane was so extreme."

"You did see. You swept it under the rug because you didn't want to upset the applecart."

"Well, other than Thane we had a nice thing going."

"Till you didn't live up to her expectations."

"To my expectations."

"Plus the other issue."

"Meaning?"

"Meaning you like living in Connecticut?"

"I'm okay."

"Bullshit, you hate it. Adjusting to rural life had to take some toll on you. To deal with the isolation, the silence at night, the lightning storms, the pollen, the poison ivy, the fucking grasshoppers."

"And yet I think I would miss Connie."

"Aha—now we're getting it. You have a morbid fear of facing life alone. My god, what are you so afraid of that you need a body in bed with you at night?"

"I'm afraid of time and space. Of light years. If I wake up in the middle of the night my mind starts running big numbers. Like this meteor that travels at a million miles an hour—imagine a million miles an hour—and after a thousand years at that speed it will only have traveled one and a half light years. That's the kind of size we're dealing with here. I lay on my pillow and try to get my mind around those figures and I'm scared."

Baum's anxiety did not fit Freud's playbook. Loving parents, nice household, never accidentally stumbled upon them in flagrante delicto and mistook it for a violent assault. Good student, popular in school, nice friends, hovered with them after class over a phonograph listening to Mozart, Heifetz,

Duke Ellington, good music, pizza, sushi, the usual, summers at the beach, the ocean, the bay within short walking distance from the rented bungalow on Michigan Street, the Selvins in the bungalow across the street with Eddie's sixteen year-old sister Noel, a man's name on a girl but she was pretty and Baum would have married her if he wasn't eight years old. Of course, the movie houses, the TV programs, the presents on birthdays and Christmas or Chanukah, but what's the difference to a kid as long as there's merchandise?

No, there was no reason for growing up with a fear of loneliness because he was never left alone, never traumatized, never dumped with maids, never abandoned, never lost on the subway. And yet, for whatever reason at a very young age, a shadow had already descended on Baum when it became clear to him that the tiny space he took up in the grudging universe, the universe would one day want back.

"I need someone," he babbled aloud to himself as he sped along the highway toward a bed with Connie in it. "She gets angry with me more easily lately. You listening?"

"What?"

"I'm saying she gets angry. She's got a temper. Am I boring you?"

"Sometimes you do bore me, Asher. If she's so damn dissatisfied, why doesn't she just leave you?"

"I'm sure she might if the right opportunity presented itself. You know, inertia is one of the strongest forces in physics. And I'm sure she's had her little adventures."

"You may be sure but I'm not."

Baum recalled that night in January two years ago. He had driven into Manhattan during a snowstorm to see his dermatologist, Doctor Gill. He had become convinced the two black spots on his back were melanomas. He first discovered them when he got into bed to read before going to sleep and Connie had said, "What are those things on your back?" He slept in his T-shirt and it had ridden up when she noticed them. It took some twisting and turning to see them in the mirror but when he managed it, both his stomach and his heart went into high alert.

"Oh my god," he mumbled and you could hear the adrenaline roaring forth.

"How long have you had them?"

"I don't know. Have you seen them before?"

"I don't think so."

"Gee," he said, by now his only thought was how he was going to react to the chemo.

"It's probably nothing," Connie said, providing him with a nanosecond of relief before dropping the other shoe dashing his hopes. "They don't look like bites." It was about eleven at night. Too late to call Dr. Gill but he could text her, show her photos of the spots. He had Connie use his phone and photograph the two black spots. Looking at the photos Baum saw them clearly for the first time without twisting his neck and spine to get only a half look. No question in his mind, they met the description of the melanoma he so often googled—dark, raised, irregular borders. In a major wax he sent the photos to Doctor Sandra Gill hoping to get a reassuring text back. After a few minutes his phone rang and the dermatologist asked him how long he had the spots. He said he wasn't sure, waiting for some words of reassurance that perhaps stem cell or immunotherapy might work, and he wouldn't need harsher treatment.

"Can you come in tomorrow?" Doctor Gill said.

"What time?" Baum asked. Could he come tomorrow? He could get in the car and come in now in his pajamas.

"I'm very busy but I'll fit you in."

"I'll be there at noon," Baum said and hung up convinced that making the effort to fit him in was a sure sign that she saw the two black spots as an emergency. Of course, he had a bad night tossing and turning, nervous, unable to fall asleep, lying in the dark running through a dozen scenarios that included loss of his hair, his cremation, his soul floating through the ether to where? To where the poet Philip Larkin said was nowhere. Finally, a little sleep came to Baum and with it a dream where he had a very aggressive cancer that spread to his lymph nodes, his pancreas, his brain, then to the leather chair in his study and to his bureau and all his cashmere sweaters. He awakened in a sweat. It was morning and he checked and the spots were still there. He shaved, showered and took some tea and toast, got the car and drove into the falling snow which blew against his windshield all the way.

What's with Baum?

He arrived for his appointment early and leafed through some magazines. In one, the people of Haiti were being slaughtered, in another the Ukrainian people were being slaughtered, in Gaza people were being slaughtered. He put down the magazine and picked up the daily newspaper where one did not have to fly so far to be slaughtered as there were plenty of locals being shot, stabbed or pushed onto the subway tracks. Not to mention massacred in shopping malls and schools. We were definitely a failed species, up from the apes but not enough to make a substantial difference. After much self-inflicted suffering in the waiting room, he heard his name called. His moment had arrived.

Doctor Gill was young, pretty, always in a tight skirt and white jacket. She was married to another doctor who worked at Mount Sinai. That's all he knew. That, and on several occasions less critical than that day, he had wondered what it would be like to sleep with her. The sexual signal goes round and round endlessly like radar on a ship. And always unexplainable. She didn't take insurance and that fact aroused him. Go figure. Dr. Gill took one look at the two black spots, which she ominously referred to as lesions, and said, "The photos looked much worse. They're both keratoses. Nothing. I'll take them off and biopsy them but it's just protocol. I can tell you they're nothing."

In that moment, for him, the earth revolved in movie slow motion. He would live. In his mind he had come this close to a fatal diagnosis but managed to cheat the hangman once again, a triumph for all the hypochondriacs of the world. He watched Dr. Gill wiggle away in her short skirt and took a deep breath. In five more minutes, he was out on the New York streets, claiming his automobile but now the blizzard predicted by the hysterical weathermen on TV was in full regalia. He started to drive back to Connecticut but it was murder. He phoned Connie and said safest was to stay in town at their apartment and come home tomorrow. She agreed and then laid on him that his brother Josh had come to visit and for the same reason he would be forced to stay over in the guest room.

Baum understood but when he hung up and got back to their pied-à-terre the picture began to take shape in his mind. The country house, isolated in the snow, smoke puffing out of the chimney as in a Grandma Moses painting. Josh alone with his wife. Good-looking, virile Josh with a lovely creature whose sex activity had been tapering off with her husband for a while now. The flakes falling softly, drinks, the fireplace blazing away, Josh with a libido that should go into the *Guinness Book of World Records*. Would he resist? Could he? Could anyone under similar circumstances?

With that he went downstairs to the garage of the building and got his car. The attendant thought he was nuts.

"Where to Mister Baum?" he asked.

"Connecticut."

"Oh, I don't think so," the man said.

"We'll see."

What's with Baum?

A little past the George Washington Bridge he turned back. Later on he lay awake in the New York apartment wondering if it would matter to Josh that he was his brother. Would he allow this platinum opportunity to go wasted? Would the morality issue, for Josh, trump the surge of his blood toward those predictable destinations? He envisioned them over dinner, his sexy wife with a glass of burgundy, his brother with a macho five o'clock shadow staring into her eyes. How could there be any other outcome? Always with Connie, alcohol loosened her up quickly. Two glasses of red wine and she was ready for bungee jumping. She was always up for any new experience. He considered himself lucky none of their friends had ever suggested a safari or LSD. Knocking off Josh in the sack would be just like her, especially the way things were going lately. "Just one more glass. My god, have we finished the whole bottle?"

When Baum finally did return home the next day he couldn't help thinking there was something between his brother and his wife like two cats who ate the same canary. He couldn't be sure, but when Josh said goodbye he thought he noticed a look they gave one another. But maybe he was imagining it.

"So yes," he said, alone in his car, now recalling the incident as he neared Connecticut. "This lovely Asian girl was so flattering, so enthused over my writing, so charming, and yes, I kept staring at her crossing and uncrossing her legs. You had to be there to appreciate it and from Connie all I get is flack and how brilliant her male model–looking son is and his first novel is short-listed. God, I hate that kid."

"Here we go again."

"So, when we were saying goodbye after one of the most enjoyable interviews I've had in ages, I took her by the shoulders and kissed her. That's when she pushed me and I lost my balance."

"Okay, so the girl wasn't making it up."

"But did she have to make it the centerpiece of the article?"

"You handed the story to her on a silver platter. She's a journalist. You gave her a real climax to her interview."

"She didn't think my prose was bloated before I hit on her. She liked that my play was about something. Not just escapist."

"And then you ruin it by attacking her."

"And she changes her mind about my books."

"You walked into that one, Asher."

"I didn't know what I was doing. I'm telling you I'm not myself lately."

He was still bantering back and forth, pleading for understanding, when he arrived home and finally pulled himself together. It was late and Connie was asleep. He tiptoed into the bedroom, careful not to wake her up.

He looked at her lying there, her lap throw having crept aside leaving her bare leg provocatively exposed, her face as unspoiled by time as the night they met, even softer in repose than in waking, when she could be a terror. She once threw a fork at him during a spat. Naturally over Thane. He had purchased a few expensive ounces of beluga for Connie on Mother's Day. He envisioned the two of them or even her alone feasting on it. Thane ate it all as she had given it to him because she knew he liked it. Baum was annoyed and said he had bought it for her. She happily sacrificed it for Thane. This led to words, more words, loud words, louder, nastier, and finally as Baum exited the room angrily she picked up a fork and threw it at his back. With time her temper cooled but she never apologized. Months later when he came back from Manhattan with a small jar of herring in cream sauce which he bought at Barney Greengrass and was a favorite of his, he hid it in his sock drawer and ate it alone all at once.

Years ago, she would have liked it if he had awakened her. She would have enjoyed the spontaneous lovemaking. Now if he woke her she'd be cranky at the intrusion between her and whichever leading man was starring that night in her dreams. She wouldn't be able to get back to sleep, a problem she never had before. She had once awakened him in Bora Bora so they could share the sunrise and as Hemingway might say, "the lovemaking that dawn was good and true. It was fine lovemaking and after they lay there resting, they did it again." Thane had remained asleep in the next room and she had been careful not to moan too loud for fear of waking him.

Right from the start Thane was always hovering. She took him to Bora Bora. "I want him to see the colorful fish in the clear blue ocean," she explained. She brought him along to Venice. "He won't believe Venice, nobody does the first time. I can't wait to see his face." Thane traveled with them to Athens, to Istanbul. He loved the Blue Mosque but he was most fascinated by those daggers with the huge emeralds. In Spain Thane got sick. He had to have his appendix out. You would have thought they were in the remotest jungles of the Amazon with only medicine men. Connie was weak with anxiety. Of course, in San Sebastian it was done perfectly and the next day he was prancing around the lobby of the hotel ordering dinner in the restaurant.

"Isn't that sophisticated?" Connie said breathlessly. "He's developed a taste for foie gras and truffles. When I was twelve I'd never heard of truffles." At the hotel in Paris the following year Baum said, "You really think he needs a massage?"

"He enjoys it when the masseuse comes to the room with his table," Connie said.

"And a pedicure?" Baum said.

"You will admit he's gorgeous," she said. And Baum would have had to admit it. But he didn't because Thane was by then well on his shit list. Yes, the kid was definitely beautiful in a certain way. "And so bright," Connie said in those early years when they traveled a lot because she loved to sightsee and educate Thane, and while Baum made little money, she had no issues being the family bank. Down the line during arguments the issue of money came up only once and he thought it must have bothered her more than she let on.

What's with Baum?

"I had his IQ tested," Connie said with pride about her son. "They were amazed at Harvard. He was around one sixty which is the stratosphere but I could have told them that." Try as he did Baum could not seem to bond with Thane who considered his birth father a brilliant and great architect and Baum an intruder who couldn't seem to keep his hands off his mother. It was a fact that both his parents were extremely bright and beautiful and here was this Baum character full of highfalutin ambition and mediocre product. What does she see in him? Thane wondered. An artist? So where is it? How did this clown suddenly become my stepfather? Baum had tried to be a good stepfather but couldn't seem to score with Thane. And for Connie there was nothing too good for her son. Did that kid need a mattress that cost over fifty grand? Baum asked himself. Thane's sore back was the rationale. His father had mild scoliosis, and Connie didn't want Thane to grow up with a crooked spine. This kid's got to be blond, erect like in the Hitler Youth. And did Connie think maybe it was possible she was spoiling him by treating the kid to a Rolex for his fourteenth birthday just because he made some noise about having his heart set on one?

Thane and Baum argued often as Thane grew up but it wasn't the kind of arguments he had with Amnon Weinstock, the new tambourine player for The White Chocolate Dandies. These arguments were not disputations between honorable men who disagreed. They were personal attacks, ostensibly about politics and literature but really opportunities to slip in little hostile commercials sponsored by a frustrated older artist and a smug youth. Baum found Thane more and more taken with himself over the years. Once, when the family went to the movies to see *Persona*, the Ingmar Bergman film, Baum was moved by it. Thane found it obscure, pretentious, artsy, a bore. When Baum touted Faulkner's *The Sound and the Fury*, Thane found it just okay, nothing more. Thinking he was coming up with a sure thing for a thirteen-year-old boy to enjoy, Baum told Thane to read *The Catcher in the Rye*. Thane hated it, dismissing the protagonist as a chronic complainer.

Now with the phenomenal success of his first novel, the Thane-Baum chemistry had only worsened. Thane resented having to defend his success against accusations of middle-brow commercialism by what he saw as an embittered failed artist who had somehow managed to fool his mother.

"Is it any wonder every woman falls in love with Thane?" his beaming mama would say. "I could if the law allowed."

The most sickening thing to Baum was that Thane's recent celebrity status enabled him to make a public offer to trade places with a scientist held hostage by the Russian government. Baum called it blatant grandstanding bullshit as Thane had to know the State Department would never allow it. A safe but self-aggrandizing offer, Baum grumbled. "The little putz," Baum told Sheila Wasserman, his cousin whose brother had died in the Vietnam War. "Trying to play hero."

What's with Baum?

The clincher was one day when Thane had just handed in his manuscript to the publisher and Baum overheard a conversation between the boy and his mother. The three were playing Scrabble and drinking wine on a rainy summer night. Baum excused himself and said he was going upstairs. The other two continued to play, not realizing Baum had detoured to the kitchen to grab a little taste of something before retiring. He started searching for some fudge brownies when he felt a slight pain on the left side of his chest. Wondering if it might be the onset of a coronary thrombosis, he sat and rested. For some moments, all was quiet save for the voices of Thane and his mother over Scrabble. Neither realized Baum had not gone upstairs to bed but could hear every word.

"What was with him tonight?" Thane said. "His mind was not on the game. That's for sure."

"He's always in a fog when he's planning a new novel."

"Is that it? I hope not another lifeless philosophy lesson where he's every character or should I say, his ideas are."

"Sometimes I think he'd be happiest teaching at one of the universities," Connie said, "but he won't settle for that."

"You mean you won't." Thane drank more wine and fought being honest versus kind.

"You're right. I'm a bitch."

"The problem is you overestimated him."

"Your mother's a spoiled woman. Very demanding."

"Time to admit your mistake," Thane said. "He's medio-cre with half-baked ideas. Everything he says has been said a hundred times before and so much better. All those unan-swerable questions come alive with great writers. With him, it's all homework and moralizing. I'm not saying he doesn't have a certain glibness with words which is great for Scrab-ble but that's not literature. Am I being too frank?"

"You never liked Asher, did you? Right from the start," his mother asked. She was now modestly inebriated from sipping Chambolle-Musigny the last hours.

"May I be permitted to just say what's been on my mind since we've come this far?"

"I know you never liked him. You don't have to rub it in."

"He's a loser, Mother. Unworthy of you. I don't know what you ever saw in him. Compared to Dad he's a cipher. I felt it from the first and time has proven me right. You brought this up so I'm telling you. I try to be respectful to him for your sake but he's a boob, a punchline."

Now it was his turn to sip again, to fortify himself for the remainder of his unpleasant monologue. All the while Baum sat silently listening, distracted from his chest pain, which would prove to be indigestion. A boob, a punchline. So, this is what this supercilious wunderkind had reduced him to. Not a noble suffering writer but a nudnick. He wanted to run into the other room and smack him across the face.

"Your stepfather was once a very charming, intelligent man," came Connie's unsteady voice. "In certain ways he can still be rather brilliant and when you say a glib way with words—he has more than that. I fell in love with a piece he had written on the Holocaust. He has deep feelings about life. He had done some short stories that suggested real talent. I believed he could write a great book one day. He seemed to me to have so much potential."

"And I find you mistake dark for deep. He's cynical. It's easy to be pessimistic with no solutions. There's no joy, no redemption. Who wants to read through hundreds of pages to be told we need to delude ourselves to get through it all? Not me. It's a curse. He won't settle for less than great. No one needs his warmed-over *Karamazov*. Or a derivative five hundred pages of his other favorite writer, Kafka," Thane said.

"He was ambitious, and he cares about humanity. He articulated his ambition very well when we met. He was very impressive and I had come off two rocky marriages."

"You mean he talks a good game."

"I only wish you two got along better."

"He resents me because I see through him. I only hope when my book comes out it will give you the joy and fulfillment you deserve. You know I owe so much to you."

This candid appraisal of Baum did little in the latter's eyes to endear him to his stepson. The snotty little *vontz*, Baum thought. I can't stomach him and I hated his book; pretentious from cover to cover. And I don't care what the press says. Yes, it's a very gripping premise and yes, the characters are unique but it panders to the fashion of the day. But fashions change and his book, ingenious as it may be, will be left in the dust bin of history, the remaindered bin.

Baum pictured Helen Hokinson biddies at the book club, sighing over it and finding meaning where there was none. Now they were coming to film a feature on how great this new flavor of the month was for a Sunday morning TV news show. Baum would be expected to sing his praises, glamorize his work habits, his depth of thought, his charm. In a bad movie he would turn to the camera and excoriate the fatuous fake. He's a spoiled little narcissist, a second-rate talent trading on hysterical reviewers and a dumbed-down public. But this was not a movie and he would not shoot the boy down. He would not tell the world of the mistake they were making and that one day his book would be written about the way Fenimore Cooper was written about by Mark Twain.

Baum drifted off to sleep and given the anxieties of his life one would have thought he'd dream of spiders or his standard recurring nightmare where he was tied up with duct tape over his mouth and kicked to death by a jury of his peers. But no, his dream that night was rather lovely. In it his parents were celebrating an anniversary, and Baum was very moved seeing them kiss and as in love as deeply now as when they met. For their anniversary present Baum dreamed he bought them a radio, an antique radio from years ago, and when they turned it on it still worked, only it picked up shows and tunes from out of the past long gone, and as Baum slept, one could almost make out a vague smile on his face as he was seeing his mother and father hold each other listening to an old Philco tuned in to the *Make Believe Ballroom*.

When he woke the next morning reality had oozed its insidious ichor back in like rubber cement. It was an overcast autumn day, actually the kind of weather he liked. Baum hated sunny days. Apart from the fact he was worried ultraviolet rays were carcinogenic, he did not like to see the world lit harshly. Soft gray light was lovely but everything and everybody exposed too brightly was not romantic and he always preferred rain which he loved.

He and Connie ate breakfast silently engrossed in their individual copies of *The New York Times*, her copy on a laptop and his on his cell phone, now and then venturing trivial comments on the day's havoc or political ineptitude. He tried to tell her of his dream but she was wrapped up in a story about the gang rape of a Brazilian girl. He went back to an account of a man on the street struck with a hammer by a total stranger at random. Their diverse attentions met only over an 1821 law still on the books that if broken could cost the perpetrator a year of imprisonment. They were both fascinated by the fact that it was a federal crime for a non-dentist to make false teeth and ship the dentures across state lines. Connie wondered if anyone actually served time for it. And Baum thought it was great fodder for some humorist to use for a New Yorker casual. He might have tried it if he had the time to digress from the book he was thinking about, which was anything but amusing and was about the Inquisition torturing Galileo to force him to recant his scientific findings.

The item led to a discussion of American laws, criminal justice, and eventually capital punishment. Connie was unequivocally against it; Baum, less certain. A man slaughters five children in a family, he reasoned. What if it gives a minuscule measure of comfort to the parents to know the killer was hanged? She argued the duty was to society and not to vengeful parents, and no society can condone the taking of lives for punishment. The debate went on through coffee and corn muffins, and nothing was settled. For his part, on any conflicting issue he could never seem to feel certain of his ground no matter how well thought out his position was. He was a master of self-doubt.

The truth was, that morning he was just happy there was no coverage of an author suddenly making an aggressive lunge at a female journalist after interviewing said author.

After breakfast they went their ways, she to look at some newly acquired pictures of dogs. Connie was determined to have a dog despite the fact that she knew he was not crazy about pets. She argued that a Doberman would be very protective and while she was not the least bit nervous about burglars, she knew he was a little paranoid and might appreciate a watchdog. He said Dobermans reminded him of the Gestapo and he was sure they were bred to be anti-Semitic.

She switched to a Golden Retriever. He found a Retriever bright, friendly and loyal but in the end, still a dog. Four legs and it barked. Not for him. She had even made some noise about raising Poodles and entering dog shows. She said he should do a little investigating on the breeds because eventually she meant to get one. Baum's feelings on the matter were to be as usual written off as the kvetching of a crank. "For god's sake," she said impatiently, "who doesn't like dogs?"

He paced across the lake thinking that it wasn't that he absolutely hated all dogs but with his life coming undone, the last thing in the world he needed was a panting pooch staring up at him. As a child he longed for a dog desperately, primed by their lifesaving feats of courage, bravery and superintelligence as seen in movies. When his parents finally succumbed and bought him a Spaniel, he found it burdensome, demanding, stupid and if anything, cowardly. When he stopped to think about it, he was not an animal lover. Wild jungle cats he found beautiful and magnificent but a hound on a leash or a parrot in a cage or god help us, guppies, forget it. Pets were not for Baum. The point is, Connie didn't care. It was her way or the highway. The tension between them had over the years become a tangible thing just as empty space is not really empty, so the tension they lived in was alive with quantum particles.

"Suddenly, it's a dog. She knows how I feel but I don't get a vote. Yes, I can insist but it will lead to yet another fight that will only lead to a fight much louder and finally a fight no longer about Poodles or Dobermans or Golden Retrievers but about ways we've let each other down." Baum was right. Dogs would open the door to accusations of insensitivity, missed moments, unimaginative sex, loneliness in each other's presence. Who knew? But it would definitely no longer have anything to do with Fido or Rover.

Now, across the lake on the driveway of the house a car pulled up and it was Thane and his girlfriend. The one he touted so enthusiastically; the one Connie thinks is perfect for him. Baum couldn't see her at this distance but was sure she would be another cookie-cutter model that was astonishing in a bikini but less than scintillating.

"Some of them are quite intelligent," he said to himself.

"Yes, a neurosurgeon, wasn't one?"

"Yes, with the kind of body that only comes to men in dreams."

"Christ, what the hell do they see in him?"

"He's only got everything going for him and now he's selling the movie rights."

"Where did you read that?"

"I read it in one of the gossip columns."

"A movie deal for that book? I shouldn't be surprised. It's a commercial story."

"It's got a great plot and colorful characters."

"It's a movie I won't be seeing."

"Believe me, they'll survive without your fifteen dollars." Asher made a few deprecating remarks to himself just as

What's with Baum?

Connie exited her house across the water and Baum could see much hugging as she clearly enjoyed Thane's girlfriend. I suppose I have to meet her and show interest, Baum thought. Connie waved to Baum to join them. Baum thought, She couldn't care less I'm here struggling over the structure of my new novel. I'm a working writer who cares about literature, but Thane is here so drop everything and maybe he'll tell me what to say to the TV interviewer. He and Connie will vet my praise to see if it's lavish enough.

When Baum circled the pond and wandered back to the house, Thane, his girlfriend Sam, and Connie had moved indoors. Connie was fixing a frozen mochaccino for her son while the prodigy was selling his date on the mixture as pure ambrosia "the way Mom makes it."

When Baum entered and set eyes on Thane's date, he was taken aback. It wasn't just that she was beautiful but she bore a very strong resemblance to his ex-wife Tyler, the love of Baum's life. Sam was farm fresh, a knockout like Tyler with no makeup, great on the natch. Baum couldn't stop staring. The resemblance to Tyler was unmistakable. Like Tyler, Sam looked like she'd be equally at home with a martini in a penthouse or lying back on a haystack in Iowa. She wore a white cotton dress and Baum thought it's Tyler, the smile, the big eyes, the straight blonde hair.

"What are you staring at?" Connie said as she came into the room from the kitchen with two frozen mochaccinos and noticed her husband standing there tasered.

"Oh, I'm sorry. I was just trying to remember a line of poetry," he lied clumsily. "'Begotten by despair upon impossibility'—I seem to have read that."

"Andrew Marvell," Sam said. "Very romantic poet."

By now his face turned so hot you could have cooked meat on it.

"Sam, this is Asher," Thane said, introducing them. "I told you about him."

I'll bet he did, thought Asher. Probably placed the knife directly between my shoulder blades.

"You're his father," Sam said.

"Stepfather," Baum was quick to say, helplessly shifting into Awkward Baum and then Insecure Baum. The Four Horsemen of the Baum Apocalypse included also Panicky Baum and Hysterical Baum.

"Sam Taylor," she said, extending her hand.

"Why does that name ring a bell?" Baum said.

"Probably because Sam works for Thane's publisher," Connie said, giving out the drinks. "Did you want anything, Asher? Hot water and lemon?"

"No, I'm fine." Somewhere Baum had read hot water and lemon broke down the toxins and, in an attempt to live forever, he added the mixture to his assorted nostrums. Both Connie and Thane made fun of him for it.

"Thane didn't tell me you were planning a new novel," Sam said.

"Well, I'm not too deeply into it," Asher said.

God knows what Thane did or didn't tell her, he thought. He probably told her about my nervous breakdown. I'm sure he exaggerated it.

"I'd love to hear more about your novel if you're up to it," she said. "I work for Thane's publisher. I very much enjoyed your last one."

"You read it?"

"I read everything. I couldn't understand the critical reaction to it. Probably because some of the ideas were too threatening to deal with. I admired your courage."

At that moment, sweating out the four hundred agonizing pages over the past two brutal two years was suddenly all worth it.

"How do you like the mochaccino?" Thane asked Sam.

"Delicious," she said.

"C'mon," Thane said. "I never really showed you around the grounds." And then like rising in the morning with an unmotivated feeling of well-being, Baum came out of his trance and the young lovers were off to wander the woods and turning leaves.

"She's the one girl he's brought home I really think is right for him," Connie said.

"Yes?"

"I tried to introduce you to her last time she was here, but you were too busy writing a nasty letter to the *Times of London*. She's lovely, bright, very connected in the literary world. She could well make him happy and also make a real contribution to his career. Did you give anymore thought to a dog? Now I'm leaning back to a Doberman." At this moment his mind was as far from the animal world as Neptune from Perth Amboy. She is the second coming of Tyler was all that Baum could think. He hadn't had a rush of serotonin in many years, never believed it could come again and half hoped it wouldn't. Connie left the room, the house, took the car and drove into New Milford to get some groceries. Thane loved lobsters and maybe the fish market would have some left if she got there on time. Baum sat on the sofa and breathed. That's all he did, just breathed. He was feeling a mysterious buzz.

"Are you nuts?" he suddenly said aloud.

"Why nuts?"

"You let yourself get mired in nostalgia for a woman who broke your heart."

"She reminds me so much of Tyler. Not just how she looks but her way of standing, of expressing herself. I look at Sam and see Tyler."

"Asher—"

"Don't Asher me. I'm telling you, she's Tyler behind the eyes. Same story the deeper you look."

The story of Baum and Tyler would have made a good movie or maybe he should say a bad Hollywood movie. It had all the elements of a cheesy rom-com; all it lacked was a commercial ending. Baum was well over his divorce from Nina when Tyler came along. He lived in a small apartment on Seventy-Eighth Street, between Park and Lexington. In those days, many townhouses once lived in by single families had been broken up into multiple dwellings resulting in an endless variety of new-fangled apartments, some charming, some awkward, expensive but affordable. Baum's flat was not bad. It had a nice view out the back window of somebody's tree-lined garden and had a fireplace. It rented for eight fifty a month and today would cost thousands for the same two and a half rooms.

It was on a July Fourth weekend. Manhattan, and certainly the Upper East Side, was empty, its upscale population off to the Hamptons or Martha's Vineyard or Europe. Anyplace but the humid ninety-degree city streets. And then there was Baum and those few cement addicts who like Manhattan in the summer. These souls relished the drop in traffic and accessibility of everything from restaurants to museums to Broadway shows. Baum hated all the clichéd vacation spots, liked Manhattan in the summer as long as his air conditioner worked. By Labor Day he had had enough quiet time and welcomed back the return of the dwellers and life with its promising chaos. He had once been persuaded to be a guest of friends in East Hampton. He found the drive long and boring, the traffic so paralyzed he literally inched his way there. The house was large and opulent facing the sea and he was given a lovely room, but he found the bed sheets clammy and the relentless sound of the waves pounding the beach made it hard for him to sleep. Oddly, the roaring urban cacophony never disturbed his rest; not the police sirens, the ambulances or fire trucks, the mitzvah mobiles or jackhammers fixing potholes at all times of the day or night. But the soothing lull of the Atlantic doing its thing kept him awake.

In the Hamptons he was up and dressed at 6:00 a.m. and did enjoy a walk on the cool white sand. Alone on the endless coastline, the huge dawn sky gray and moody, the vast ocean, up and back in its rhythm signifying only that time moves in one direction, naturally his thoughts turned to the eternal and from there to the religious. It was here, under these conditions, if ever God's plan was meant to become apparent, this was the setting. Staring out into the horizon he awaited some sign. When no message emerged, no sacred instructions to go along with his ineffable intuition of "something greater" materialized and God was a no-show he began to miss the city where intimations of immortality were scarce, but in trouble you could dial 911. So much for the divine tease, a hustle for suckers.

There were a few parties his hosts took him to later in the day, populated by characters that would have delighted any caricaturist. "Rose Kimmel Shows Off Her New JAR Earrings" from The Barbeque at Amagansett, a series of plates by William Hogarth. Plate #2: "Sidney Kantor the CEO of a Hedge Fund Throws a Frisbee to His Dog." Plate #3: "Max Koch Recommending to Edith Klein She Sue Her Plastic Surgeon." Plate #4: "A Drunk Gets Guacamole on the

Gillmans' Rothko." Plate #5: "Fran Bigman Telling an Actor She Doesn't Believe Any of the Allegations."

As Baum left the party and walked to his car he envisioned himself not in caricature but in a painting with his hands clapped over his ears, mouth wide open and signed by Edvard Munch.

When Baum arrived back in Manhattan after a bumper-to-bumper ride the length of a *Queen Mary* crossing, he undressed to shower and prepare for bed when, to his horror, he noticed two black dots on his leg. His first thought, as usual, was melanoma, and he ran to get his dermatologist on the phone. Then he noticed the dots did not have the features he memorized from the warning signs card in his skin doctor's office. It was at that moment in one heart-stopping jolt that he realized there were ticks embedded in his skin. His scalp froze, hair standing at attention like her majesty's Coldstream Guards. Frantic, his head throbbing, he scanned his body thoroughly to see if there were any other intruders and was mortified to find a third creature in his back. Fighting off a typhoon of panic, he remembered that he had once read not to try to extract ticks with tweezers as one can pull the head off but leave the body embedded. The proper way was to light a match, then blow it out and touch the hot tip to the exposed part of the bug causing it to scamper out.

Hysterically he scoured the grounds for matches. He didn't smoke but wait, the fireplace. There were matches in the copper pot on the hearth. He ran to get them, lit one and touched it to the beasts' heads. Miraculously they withdrew exactly as the manual said they would. The problem came with the one on his back which he could not reach no matter how he squirmed and convoluted. Curse of curses, he had to go upstairs and ask a neighbor to perform the gruesome act. Everyone in the building was away for the weekend except one housebound old lady, Mrs. Melnikoff, a sour crone to be sure. Melnikoff was ninety and compromised with dimming sight and doing the best she could with a couple of antiquated hearing aids. First, he scared the poor thing out of her wits by ringing her bell over and over at this late hour and then explaining to a near-deaf nonagenarian the complexities of his plight. She didn't know what a tick was and thought his charades indicated St. Vitus' Dance. Over and over he outlined what needed to be done, and when he finally removed his shirt she let out a scream. After a few pitiful tries with her shaking hand that tortured Baum over and over with hot match tips, she finally hit the mark. Baum could have wept with gratitude. He made a mental note to send a big bouquet of flowers, returned to his apartment, poured himself a full tumbler of port, and got the first peaceful sleep he'd had in days.

And so, he had sworn off venturing away from his favorite zip code during summer months, preferring the insect-free dog days at home with his Vornado dialed to high cool. He knew a few people who stayed in town, but even they went away most weekends. The only problem was that while he chose the streets of Manhattan in July and August, he was also lonely. One July Fourth with the Upper East Side desolate like the aftermath of a neutron bomb attack, he finished the morning's work on his novel and broke for lunch. It was a "three-H day": hot, humid, hazy, the kind of weather New Yorkers hate most. Nothing in the fridge, he decided to go out to Madison Avenue to the deli, get himself a prosciutto and cheese sandwich and a beer and maybe a cherry Danish.

He left his apartment, walked slowly the two short blocks to the store hoping to avoid a massive heat stroke and entered its delightful cool white space. He ordered his sandwich and browsed the *schnecken* in search of a suitable postprandial sweet. It was then that he noticed a young woman, terrifically beautiful in that unspoiled peasant way that unfailingly worked its voodoo on him, a cheerful round face with big eyes, no makeup, straight blonde hair, silver hoops in her ears, sandals and a short white summer cotton dress. Baum would later describe her curvaceous shape as having achieved "immaculate succulence." This potent combination of small miracles was for Baum like a cocktail with a Mickey Finn in it, and watching her stretch to reach for a jar on a high shelf transported him to the outer edge of the Andromeda Galaxy. What is it with these white cotton summer dresses? he wondered. Are they laundered in pheromones?

He said, "Can I help you get that down?"
She said, "I'd love that."

He performed the gallant act with the same bravado as Sir Walter Raleigh draping his cape over the mud puddle.

"Thanks so much," she said as he stared at her face, his eyes spinning like Catherine wheels. "I think we must be the only two people left in the city," she added.

"Yes," he said, "I kind of like that idea." Suddenly he heard himself say "kind of." He should have said "I like the idea of that" and edited out the nauseatingly cute "kind of."

"Me too," she said.

Then he couldn't come up with anything. This writer, this wordsmith, novelist, the man who stood ready to match sentences with the authors of *Crime and Punishment* and *The Trial* couldn't think of how to keep the conversation going after the vacuous "I kind of like that." She walked to the counter where the counterman handed her her order.

"Here's your shrimp salad. Will that be all?"

"And this honey," she said.

Baum stood like Markham's hoe man, stolid and stunned, a brother to the ox as she doled out the money, picked up her salad in its plastic container and vanished through the door into the sizzle of the city. At last Baum came to life and blinked, regretting his dumbstruck inaction. He bolted to the counter, passed on the Danish and paid for his ham sandwich. He wanted to talk to that woman. He did not want her to just exit his life. Out the door in a trice, he looked in every direction, impervious to the tropical humidity, and there she was in the distance turning up the block on Seventy-Sixth

Street walking toward Fifth. He hustled after her but when he hit her street, he arrived just in time to see her walking into a brownstone. By the time he reached it and realized it was similar to his, broken into a half dozen apartments, the downstairs door was locked and she was gone. He assessed his situation, pondered his options. He looked at the names on the buzzer wondering what button he might press. Was she Dubinsky? Jethro, Leeds, Hart, Royce, Jazack? It occurred to him that he was behaving like a frantic idiot. But what does a man do when he falls in love at first sight; when he goes to buy a ham sandwich and sees a woman he'd like to spend the rest of his life looking at every morning, be cremated with and share an urn for eternity? This is a film, he thought. I am in a movie. I am framed in celluloid.

It had always been his friend Weinstock's theory that writers were more dramatic than actors. They affected certain wardrobes; tweeds with elbow patches, army jackets, turtlenecks, suede boots; they drank and smoked to excess, challenging death, they took their own lives. They were actors playing writers and here he was, a writer but in a different kind of film. He was caught in a foolish romantic comedy, cast as the hapless protagonist behaving ridiculously over a woman he didn't know; a woman who could be living with some guy or who poisoned her last three husbands. He tried ringing Hart and Jazack but no one was home. He rang Leeds and a man answered.

"Sorry, I hit the wrong bell." When he hit Royce, she answered, and he recognized her voice.

"Yes?" she said.

"Er—hi," he fumfered. "You are the lady who just bought the shrimp salad at the deli?"

"Who is this?"

"I'm the only other person in New York City this weekend. I helped you get down the honey from the top shelf."

"Oh, oh, thank you. Did I not thank you?"

"I meant to talk to you but you left the store and I saw you and saw you walk into this building."

"You followed me?"

"Not in the sense of stalking. I tried to catch up with you to continue our conversation and I saw you go into this building. Look, if I'm bothering you—I live right around the corner. My name is Asher Baum. I'm a writer. Maybe you read my book, *Despair*. Not that you necessarily would have read it but you might have. If you weren't put off by the reviews. But the French translation sold fairly well. Probably because of the existential theme."

"Who is this?"

"Asher Baum. I reached up and got the honey on the top shelf."

"Oh, oh, right. Well thank you."

"Hey look, can I interest you in lunch? I thought since we're both in the city maybe we could take the lunches we just bought to the park and eat on a bench."

"I already ate lunch."

"You ate lunch? That salad?"

"Yes."

"So fast?"

"Yes."

"My god, well, I'm out of ideas. I thought it was a nice thing. I love Central Park. Who thought you—you must have been famished."

"I'm a fast eater."

"Well, if you won't have lunch with me, will you marry me?"

"Not today. It's too hot," she said. "But I'll give you my phone number and we could have lunch another time. I'm around all summer." He took her number and called it the minute he got home five minutes later. They made a date for dinner the next night and from this unlikely beginning he experienced the best few years of his life.

They spent July and August together. The only two people left in the city or so it felt. They shared the town, took walks in the park, dined everywhere, saw every movie, visited every museum, listened to Mostly Mozart, did every show on Broadway. She was perfect for Baum. Tyler Royce, born and raised on Park Avenue, private schools, Bard College, brilliant, quick-witted. "Marriage is the death of hope," was one of her aphorisms but by summer's end they talked of becoming man and wife. She had thought about being an architect but decided in college to be an actress. When she came to the conclusion she'd never be great she tried teaching acting and then became interested in writing and sold a television script. Where her real genius lay was in two areas. She was a muse. Every man she dated or went with or slept with owed her some debt for inspiring and directing his career, criticizing his work, making it better. The painter forsook his dependence on de Kooning, the musician played "The Goldberg Variations" with greater complexity. Baum, the novelist, improved under her watch. She read his work in progress and told him what was fresh and what was stale.

She urged his already lofty ambition to aim even higher and disregard the commercial world and not read criticism, life was too short. Her approbation became the most important thing to him and just as the actor she lived with before him and the pop artist she went out with for two years and the composer she traveled to Europe with, they all took her breath and became creatively richer because of Tyler. Finally she encouraged Baum in his transition from journalism to fiction. She pushed him into his discomfort zone, to do less of what he was good at and felt safe with and take risks. Failure does not equal death. The other great genius she had was in the bedroom and there was little doubt in Baum's mind, each of the men she made love with never got those nights out of their memory.

He introduced her to his friends and she charmed them, all except his brother Josh, who couldn't say what was bothering him. "I don't know, Asher, I can't put it in words."

"What do you mean you don't know?"

"She's smart, she's great looking, fun to talk to but…"

"But, but—but what? What kind of mystical vibe are you getting about her?"

"I'm just saying why do you have to rush to get married?"

"What rush? We've been going together nearly a year. Since when is a year a rush?"

"Uh-huh," Josh said flatly but all Asher could coax from him was a tepid concession.

"And she's very tuned in to my writing. She calls me on it when I'm self-indulgent. Cut this, cut that. She's a born editor."

"I guess," Josh said maddeningly, but for whatever reason even Josh couldn't explain, Baum's brother just couldn't seem to relax and totally get with the program.

After that summer, when Manhattan was an isle of joy just made for a girl and a boy, fall came, the air turned cool and smoky and New York shrugged off the heat and humidity and woke up. For many people autumn in New York is the reason they tolerate the city's indignities the other months. Autumn and spring but to die-hard New Yorkers it's autumn that sells the town. They bought logs and made love on the shag rug in front of his fireplace. They sat together on his sofa and stared for long times into the blaze, hypnotized by the flames and each other and Billie Holiday through Baum's Hitachi speakers. They socialized mostly with her friends as by now his bunch had dissipated and his misanthropy had softly flowered.

He did introduce her to Amnon Weinstock who did not
share his brother's intuitive skepticism. He met her parents,
two attractive, wealthy people from Paris where they now
lived fulfilling her father's dream. In town for a week, they all
went out together to dinners and saw shows. She met and
charmed his parents. On her deathbed his mother said Tyler
was the nicest, prettiest, smartest girl he ever went with. In
winter they loved going into Central Park in the deep snow.
Ordinarily that was something Baum would've hated but
with Tyler it was a joy. She lived mostly at his apartment but
kept hers till she didn't. She cooked occasionally but could
only make spaghetti, so they ordered in often. Sushi was their
go-to dish. When spring came to New York they decided to
marry in June. Just the two of them rode downtown to City
Hall. No big deal. They honeymooned in Chinatown over
duck wonton soup, took a larger apartment in the neigh-
borhood they loved, the Upper East Side, moved into four
rooms just off Fifth Avenue in a converted brownstone on
Seventy-Third and settled in, him to write, her to work for
a photographer.

All well and good but now comes the crazy part. She
had simply met someone, fallen in love no matter how hard
she had tried to fight it off. She decided that the high speed
of Manhattan life was finally not really for her and she was
moving to New Zealand to be with some musician whose
passion was raising sheep. They would live on his farm where
she now realized her true destiny lay. Tyler said she had to

be away from the hurly-burly of the city streets, which she'd had enough of since birth. She'd had it with the frantic glitz of Gotham and was ready to do something more useful to society like raising sheep. She felt their marriage had been lovely, perhaps too lovely and had lulled her into such a sweet, complacent existence that she wasn't growing. Baum was a terrific human being, she felt, and one day was sure to make his mark in literature if he kept working at it. This new feeling that had come over her was almost like finding religion, she explained. She admitted she had always been a mercurial type, and it's to Baum's credit that she actually believed she would be happy marrying him, a feeling she never had for any of the previous men she was involved with. She thought maybe she felt guilty because she was enjoying her life too much. It was because Baum was so great, such a fabulous individual that she had stayed with it and was determined to make the marriage work. She thought she had it all under control. And then she met Ricky Lake, a drummer who made a ton of money, quit the music world, and bought a lot of land in New Zealand. Baum should not feel bad but proud in a way that of her many ardent swains and offers of marriage, she had chosen him. Meanwhile, she was off to New Zealand to try her hand at ewes and rams.

To say that it took Baum some effort to get his mind around this turn of events is putting it mildly. For the next year it was as if he was run over by a freight train. This was a drummer in a rock group, the kind of music she detested and called eardrum-shattering noise. As for living on a farm? She was as addicted to the streets of the big city as Damon Runyon. And now she's going to raise sheep? He bellowed all this to his few friends who intervened and explained to him that suicide solves nothing. A shrink explained how they had new medications that were very effective and perhaps together they could find the right "cocktail." Prozac with an olive in it he said sarcastically. It was a hard life lesson and he wasn't exactly sure what if anything he had learned from it. There was 'the human heart is irrational' but this cliché we all knew and he didn't need it drummed in. There was 'a woman's moods are unpredictable,' but so were men's moods and worse, men were often more violent. He came to the conclusion that not every action could be explained. He thought back to see if there was something he did without realizing it. Something he did to put Tyler off. But she never complained. The cliché love fades didn't seem to apply. "And it doesn't always fade," he muttered to the total stranger on a park bench.

These thoughts went through Baum's mind as he watched Sam go off with Thane on his tour of the grounds. That night the two young people joined Connie and Baum for dinner, the table talk dominated by Thane. Everyone got to hear his takes on all matters, to savor the suspense and sacrifice of how he came to pen his masterpiece, how the brilliant premise came to him and how he shaped each character. Baum had long tuned out. What continued to puzzle him was how a woman who seemed as intelligent and sharp as Sam did not see straight through the pompous little narcissist who held court. It was clear Sam was bright, much wittier and more charming and miles more interesting than her self-confident boyfriend. And yet, there she was, on his arm, brushing the forelock of his hair back off his forehead and gushing over this current bestseller. Tyler would have dismissed Thane's book as derivative, contrived. Or would she? Was success such a potent aphrodisiac that it would have captivated her? Thane couldn't keep his hands off Sam and if she found him a boring windbag, she didn't show it. Quite the opposite. The enigma of attraction.

Meanwhile, Baum sat, sneaking guilty glances at Sam so as not to appear excessively fascinated. It was fun dwelling on her face, beautiful like Tyler's, and she seemed in tune with him on so many points, but the moment of greatest meaning to Baum was when both he and Sam agreed that the finest soup dumplings in the city were to be found at Joe's Shanghai in Chinatown. Agreement on that trivial point left Baum with a hard-to-explain pleasant feeling. When they both agreed the highly praised downtown production of *The Cherry Orchard* was lousy, it gave Baum a chance to wax eloquently on his favorite playwright. She too swore by Chekhov.

No matter when any subject wandered too far off course, Connie always brought it back to Thane, his formative years, his acclaim and general wonderfulness. How bullfighting,

expensive Swedish mattresses and the Nizam of Hyder-
abad managed to lead back to Thane and his future plans
astounded Baum. Somehow Connie would always find a
route. Once by some miracle in the universe, an off-Broadway play Baum had written, one of several ventures into
drama, came up, and it surprised him Sam had seen it, liked
it and was shaken up by its doomsday climax.

"I thought it was a good play too," Connie said, "but
audiences found it off-putting."

"It's very hard without critical support," Thane said.
"Those critics come in and tear you apart, call you an idiot
and then what chance do you have? I remember what that
guy said about your play, Asher—'That's not writing,' he
said, 'it's whining.'"

"I don't care, I thought it was courageous of you to write
it," Sam said, looking at Baum and for a few seconds it was as
if Tyler was talking to him over spaghetti, her signature dish.
After dinner Thane, Sam and Connie got into a conversation about the upcoming TV feature planned about Thane
and how to best present him in a way that would sell more
books. Baum excused himself and went out on the porch
for some fresh air. The chilly night was a pleasure after all
the self-referential arias by Thane. Baum hated long dinners.
He liked to sit down at a meal, eat, chat a bit and then have
it over. Nina used to drive him crazy at breakfast when she
would sip her orange juice and then put down the glass, chat,
pick up her fork, cut a slice of French toast, eat the one bite,

put down the fork, sip the juice, put down the glass, chat. Baum wanted to gulp his OJ, quenching his thirst in a satisfying barbaric way, knock off his toasted English and coffee and get on with his journey through life, but there was Nina, sipping and chatting, taking small bites, sitting back while their time on earth was going through a sieve. Mysteriously her twin sister did the same, but it didn't bother him when Ann did it.

"Just what the hell were you doing at dinner?" he asked himself.

"What? What was I doing? Nothing. Eating."

"You were very interested in Thane's girlfriend."

"She reminds me of Tyler."

"I can see that."

"Can I tell you something?"

"Yes."

"But this is top secret."

"Who am I going to tell?"

"I got the feeling she was a little attracted to me."

"Based on what?"

"Oh, look at him—he's so skeptical."

"You'd like to think that, but those days are over my friend. I do not think that she will sing to you."

"You're not as sensitive as I am, but I pick up on little things. Did you notice she directed so much of her conversation to me? She liked my book and she even saw one of my off-Broadway plays and liked it. And it was not an easy play to understand."

"I'm sure of that. I must say I have no patience with that avant-garde bullshit you think is so arty. You know, I'm not a Beckett fan."

"Can we not get into a discussion of our separate tastes? My point is Sam and I seemed to be on the same wavelength."

"Why? Because, she was right there with you on where in New York to get the best soup dumplings? I wouldn't read too much into that if I were you."

"And we both hated the production of *The Cherry Orchard*. She wasn't bamboozled by the rave reviews."

"So what are you saying? I hope it's not what I think."

"I'm saying nothing. It was just a nice feeling to be appreciated by this terrific young woman. Especially since she reminds me of Tyler. That's all I'm saying. It ends there."

"Okay, because she's Thane's girlfriend."

"That's a testimony to her cognitive dissonance. She likes Thane and she can also enjoy me. She's able to hold two opposing concepts in her mind at once and still function."

"Yeah, well I'd get some sleep if I were you and figure out what you're going to say to Connie when you're accused of attacking Cindy Tanaka or whatever her name is that interviewed you."

"All I'm saying is if circumstances were different, I'd go after Sam."

"That's the problem with circumstances. They are by definition, not different. That's why they're circumstances. Get my meaning?"

"Of course I would never—"

"Right. Like you never touched the Japanese girl."

"Tyler would have had Thane's number on the first date and bailed with a fake migraine."

"Can't you forget Tyler? She wrecked you."

"Yes. In the end," he said wistfully. "But I can't get over how much Sam reminds me of her."

"Remember, it's physics. Whatever pleasure you get from a relationship, there's an equal and opposite amount of pain when you're dumped."

"Could you believe Thane quoted that bum who wrote I whine?"

"Well you do whine."

"How come the poet Allen Ginsberg writes a lament called 'Howl' and he's allowed to howl but I'm not allowed to whine?"

Baum's sleep that night was deep and peaceful and full of delightful dreams except for one where he was crucified upside down in a stalled elevator. The following morning his agent called and said he had spoken with Roadhouse, a small publishing company, and they might be interested in possibly talking about his next novel. They did offbeat, controversial books and should he set up a meeting so they could hear more about his book? Baum was happy to get that news, thanked Bell for helping even though he was a tough sell. He agreed to a meeting with the publisher, Shivay Banerjee, the following day. In one way he liked the idea of being published under a label that published literary outliers and some of the book world's renegade authors.

When he told Connie she was glad Baum might find a new publisher and hid her disappointment that the man she once thought would have a career like Thane's was settling for a house specializing in out-of-the-mainstream works. No question, she had bet on the wrong horse. She sometimes felt guilt for feeling contempt for her husband. Perhaps contempt was too strong a word. Lack of respect is better put. She was annoyed with herself for having poor artistic judgment and blamed Baum for her shortsightedness. At moments when she dwelled on it for too long she might work up a head of steam toward Baum, real anger. Why she needed so badly to have creative lovers she never figured out, and she adamantly resisted all forms of psychotherapy which she lumped in with spoon bending. Her disappointment with her husband often caused her to lose patience with Baum for not acknowledging the greatness of Thane, which she put down to envy, jealousy, competitiveness.

At noon Jerry Mack, the director came up to discuss the TV puff piece on Thane and survey the location. He came with a cameraman who was forever clicking off stills. Thane and Sam were not back yet from a country fair in New Milford and Connie was eager to welcome the men and show them around. She was at her most charming and lovely as she agreed with Jerry Mack that a feature on an up-and-coming major writer could be very exciting. She couldn't have been more thrilled when Mack went on and on about what an admirer of her son's work he was and that to write a first novel with Thane's maturity at such a young age was very impressive. When she gushed in gratitude he said, "I'm just quoting everything I read." Mack stood on the lawn and surveyed the superb rural beauty.

"Your place is stunning," he said. "I grew up on a country estate but our layout was not anything like this."

"You have to see it when it snows," she said.

"Did you put that pond in or was it natural?"

"It's natural. It used to have frogs. They ate the mosquitos. Then I stocked the pond with bass so Thane could fish and the bass ate the frogs so the mosquitos came back." She laughed a little nervously.

"I recognized the location from your son's description in his book. He captured it beautifully and he used it symbolically to perfect effect."

"Yes, his insights about living kind of apart are very moving, don't you think?"

"I was knocked out by his plotting, his people. And as I said, I grew up in rural Vermont and so many of my best memories are the farm. We called it the farm, but it wasn't much of a farm although we did have some horses and pheasants. Oh, and a few chickens. Fresh eggs."

Clearly, they hit it off and talked about the joys of pine trees and woodchucks as they rambled around the acreage, Connie showing Jerry Mack every hill and rill and of course her favorite tree, a beautiful weeping spruce.

"So many beautiful spots to photograph," he said. "My cameraman is roaming around getting shots of everything."

All the while the twosome strolled through the property, Baum sat at his desk struggling with the precise word for a sentence in his novel on the Spanish Inquisition. He paused only to scan the news on the computer to see if anything appeared about his insane error in judgment with the pretty Asian journalist. He never meant it the way she thought although it's hard to misread a lunging attempt to kiss. Was I out of control? he asked himself. He wasn't sure of anything anymore except he was the only person he could talk to and sometimes even he couldn't understand himself.

His mind wandered to Sam. He hadn't laid eyes on her since dinner, except in his dreams and even in dreams couldn't always distinguish her from Tyler Royce, the former Mrs. Tyler Baum. He had awakened early, before she and Thane rose. He had breakfast with Connie who was on about how excited she was that the TV producer was as taken with the idea of an exciting feature on Thane as she was. He was following through. They had met him before but very briefly. Baum and Connie were having lunch with Thane at Café Boulud on Park Avenue when Jerry Mack who was having lunch there as well, passed their table on his way out. He stopped, introduced himself, rattled off a stream of impressive credits and said he'd love to do something on Thane whom he considered America's most promising new author.

"I just think that book is a masterpiece," he said. "The first of many I have no doubt." Tickled pink is the cliché describing Connie while Baum sat silently, unsure if it was his tomato and onion salad or the obsequious intruder that was causing his acid reflux.

"Thane and I noticed you across the room," Connie had said. "We thought you were David Beckham."

"I'm very flattered," Jerry Mack said.

A date was made for Mack to visit them in the country and discuss the project. Thane said, "It's funny to think of oneself as the subject of a news feature—like the invasion at Normandy."

Connie and Mack laughed. Baum marveled at how with a commercially successful figure any subpar attempt to be amusing passes for wit.

When Thane's agent, Lydia Frankel, heard about the encounter, she advised Thane and Connie to grab it. "He's a great producer of documentaries, very smart and tasteful. The exposure will really be a major career boost. If there's anything I can do."

So there was Baum, huddled over his yellow pads, filling them with random notes in the hopes of either working past the stuck point of his novel or giving it up and working on something else. One of his random scrawls read: "I am fifty-one and yet I learn something new every day. The problem is, what I learn each day is that what I learned the day before was wrong."

His mind kept shifting to Sam and with Sam came Tyler, and he had the banal simplistic thought: Is it possible for a person to have only one real love in life or is that the stuff of Hollywood? It had been many years since Tyler but she seemed to be like a classic movie, replayed on his mind's screen. He amused himself thinking of Sam as the sequel. He looked out the window across the lawn and there was Connie and Jerry Mack. He had noticed at breakfast that Connie had dressed rather sexy. She was a very pretty woman, youthful, graceful, damn hot. And then it occurred to him, and maybe it occurred to him because he had been so guilty over his own thoughts about Thane's girlfriend, that something might be cooking between Connie and Mack. Maybe Connie is flirting with this filmmaker as well. Maybe she's putting on a phony charm to make sure this feature about Thane gets made. Or did she get a buzz from the handsome director? And because he had unsettling ideas in his head that Sam had triggered, he started to suspect that maybe those same kind of sparks flickered in Connie's mind. And what's going on in Jerry Mack's head? Connie was a very desirable woman and it was clear that Mack had noticed that. How could he help it? Connie was selling it.

"You're projecting," he said out loud. "Your mind's all over the place."

"You're probably right. But she did seem kind of taken with this guy right when he came over to our table that day."

"Interesting. Your paranoia's gotten worse over the years."

"I'm sure Connie's cheated. Josh, Damian and who knows who else."

"But you can't be a hundred percent certain."

"No not of anything. How do you live when you can't be certain of anything?"

"Hey look out there. To me that's a little too cozy. I'd get out there if I were you and see what the hell's shaking."

Baum rose and wandered out the door to greet them as they approached the house.

"This is Jerry Mack. You remember. You met."

"Sure. At the restaurant," Baum said as they shook hands. The predictable macho handshake, Baum noted. Somewhere along the line this guy was taught a bone-crushing handshake lets people know who the alpha male is. Baum hated him as he took his hand down to let the agony of his aching knuckles abate.

"Quite a beautiful spread you have here," Mack said.

A spread, Baum thought, cowboy lingo. It's not a ranch house, there's no cattle. "Yes," Baum said. "You're seeing it at a lovely time of year."

"I invited Jerry to lunch with us," Connie said.

"Oh great, great," Baum said amiably making his bid for an Oscar. Next thing you know, he thought, I'll be sleeping on the sofa and he'll have my spot in the bed with her.

"Why don't you show him the turtles?" Connie said. "Jerry said he loves turtles. I'll go fix some drinks. What will you have, Jerry?"

"You wouldn't by any chance have any single malt scotch?" Mack said.

"Will our Glenlivet do?" Connie said.

"A woman after my own heart," Mack said. "On the money."

"It's my favorite too," she said. "And you Asher?"

"Just a little white wine."

"White wine is the drink of choice for teenage girls," Mack said meaning no harm but Baum didn't appreciate it.

Turtles. What a thrill. This schmuck likes turtles. Now I get to walk him to the little brook and see if I can find one or two of the sluggish creatures that creep about on the rocks carrying out nature's insipid plan.

As Connie left for the house, Baum noticed Mack staring at what could only be her rear end. She had the platonic ideal of a callipygian or as he once put it more crudely, her ass made a statement. Baum could only imagine what pornography had flickered across Jerry Mack's cerebral cortex clocking her exit and it didn't involve turtles.

"You have a very beautiful wife," Mack said. "And an amazing son."

"Stepson," Baum corrected him. "Yes, I'm a very lucky man."

"I'd love to get you on film talking about Thane. All your experiences with him, watching him grow as an artist, and how you've influenced him which I'm sure you have."

"Uh-huh."

"You're a writer yourself. I'm not familiar with your work although I think your wife mentioned you had great success with one of your plays in Slovenia."

"I've had some success abroad."

"Sometimes what falls flat in our native tongue comes to life in a different language."

"Yes, my work gains something in translation."

"It's interesting. Do you ever feel any competitiveness?"

"With Thane? Or Tolstoy?"

"Funny. No, I know you love him but you're both writers of novels and it's not unusual for writers to be rather cut-throat in their appraisal of one another."

"Well, I feel no competition with Thane."

Just then Mack's cell phone went off. "Excuse me, I have to take this." He answered his call and wandered off for privacy. Baum watched him gabbing into his cell next to a rose bush and wondered what it would be like to bludgeon him with a blunt instrument.

"Take it easy," he told himself.

"Sorry, but there's something about that guy that bothers me."

"You made up a whole scenario that Connie fancies him just like with your brother or the scenic designer who lives down the road."

"I can't help it. You think it's possible Connie and I could ever put the pieces back together again? Start over."

"You want my honest opinion?"

"I'm mixed up. I've got all these feelings that contradict each other. Nothing's consistent."

"'Foolish consistency is the hobgoblin of small minds.' Ralph Waldo Emerson."

"I need some consistency. I can't make it if everything's always moving along."

"That's life. The center doesn't hold."

"It doesn't, no. I keep forgetting we're a sphere, a round ball floating in space. So what the hell can I expect? You hear what I'm saying? Can I expect stability? That's a pipe dream. I am a punchline."

"You're very agitated today. Oh—shhhh, here he comes."

Jerry Mack returned.

"Sorry, that was an emergency. A thing I'm cutting on Yayoi Kusama. Another genius. Hey, were you talking to yourself?"

"Me?"

"I was very into my phone call and looked over once or twice and you looked like you were deep in conversation."

"No, no," Baum said embarrassed. "I was probably just swatting off a bee. Hate bees. More people die of bee stings than snake bites. That's a little-known fact."

Jerry Mack was staring at him, then came out of it and said, "I'm sorry I took so long."

Connie brought a glass of scotch for Jerry Mack and a white wine for her husband.

"If I have a drink before lunch, I suddenly become a party girl," she said with a smile.

"I'd like to be around for that," Mack joshed.

Baum did not relish that little exchange and the image of the blunt instrument flashed through his mind again as Connie walked back to the house in her tight jeans.

"That's all you're having?" Mack said to Baum.

"I'm worse than Connie. Alcohol goes straight to my head. Sometimes a little wine relaxes me. But rarely anything stronger."

Jerry Mack asked to see the turtles. Baum led the way to view the disgusting little reptiles, a thrill he could have lived without. While Connie fixed chicken salad sandwiches, the men strolled and sipped. That is, Baum sipped, Jerry Mack drank up. Poised over the spot, waiting to see if a creature would emerge, they spoke and with each sip, Baum's tongue loosened.

"What kind of stuff do you write?" Mack asked. "I'm so embarrassed to say I've never read anything of yours."

"It's nothing like Thane. I'm not a genius."

"Yes, Thane reminds me of some of those great old masters. Edith Wharton. Now that's a writer. Wharton, Henry James. They weren't just deep; they were fun to read."

"I'm a big fan of the Russians and of course Kafka. They were really profound. I mean people call Thane's book profound but what it actually is, is entertaining."

"Oh, he's profound all right. And not just for his age. And his style. Some of those sentences are delicious. And I mean delicious. You could serve them as hors d'oeuvres."

"You mean like Swedish meatballs?"

"Well—"

"Or deviled eggs? Jalapeno pigs in blankets? Which hors d'oeuvres are you thinking of?"

"Do I detect a little note of envy?" Mack said. "That's what I mean by writers being competitive."

"Well when you say hors d'oeuvres are you referring to baked clams?"

Illogically, Mack who had drained his Glenlivet was not a whit affected. He was sharp, steady, intense. His taste was being questioned but he stood with the majority. Baum, on the other hand, who had gone through only about three-quarters of his white wine already had a little buzz on. He had lost a number of his inhibitions, and a slightly moronic smile was beginning to settle on his face.

"I'm not saying every book has to be *Karamazov*," he said, "or *The Trial*, and I'm not saying triviality doesn't have its place."

"You think his novel is trivial?" Mack said. "I'm shocked."

"Maybe I used the wrong word," Baum said, finishing his drink. "Would you buy banal?"

"Banal? I would hardly call it banal. Every critic has mentioned the ingenuity of the plot, of its relevance to the world we live in. There's suspense, romance."

"Okay, maybe pandering is what I'm searching for."

"I can't believe you're saying these things about your son's book."

"Stepson."

"This book has been called visionary."

"I know that particular critic you're referring to. A total cretin."

"I'm stunned."

"You know of course most critics are failed writers. They're jealous or competitive. It's the only art form where the criticism uses the same medium to criticize as the artist uses to create. Think about it."

"Are you a little high?" By now the effect of the wine had Baum's bitterness firmly in its clutches.

"Can I be frank with you? I think the book stinks."

"We'd better get back," Jerry Mack said. "I see your wife waving."

They returned to the house, the walk back helping to take some edge off Baum's lightheadedness.

"Lunch is ready," Connie said, "and here comes Thane and Sam. Just in time." There was much handshaking and excitement. Sam and Thane went upstairs to freshen up before joining for lunch.

"He's so good-looking. He could have been a movie star if he was not a writer," Jerry Mack said.

"I much prefer the world of letters to the world of Hollywood," Connie said. "I know the movie business and I don't have much regard for it. I'm so glad Thane's gift is literature."

"Well, you better have a talk with your husband. He's Thane's harshest critic," Jerry Mack said good-naturedly.

"Is he?" Connie said.

"No writer, no matter how great, is above criticism," Baum said, sensing he was in trouble.

"You were knocking Thane's work?" Connie asked.

"Let's just say if your husband gave out the National Book Award, Thane wouldn't make the short list. Or the long list for that matter."

"Asher has very peculiar views of the American literary scene," Connie said. This was said as Martha might have said it about George in *Who's Afraid of Virginia Woolf?* She was staring at Baum with her two big, beautiful eyes, now two disintegration rays.

Sam and Thane joined at the lifesaving moment for Baum and everyone sat to their chicken salad sandwiches. They ate and made small talk and while Connie took some time to suppress real rage, she gradually simmered down. It was helped when Jerry Mack went on about his plans to canonize Thane with an exciting feature in which he would ask the network for more than the usual screen time. Mack told Baum they would talk and review their different opinions before he would be asked to be interviewed. Much was made of Jerry Mack's reputation and his various documentaries.

Connie, Thane and Mack huddled over ideas for the project, Sam told Baum the county fair was sweet but not very interesting. He let it slip that he would be going into Manhattan the next day on some business and she said, "You're going into the city? Could I bum a ride? I have a meeting I can't get out of."

"Sure. What time?"

"My meeting's at eleven o'clock," she said.

"Perfect."

It was by no means perfect but the thought of spending time with Sam was so very appealing that he would move his appointment around. After a long lunch Jerry Mack thanked everyone and sped off in his BMW but not before taking Connie's cell number in case he had to reach her regarding the show. Sam had some business calls to make and Thane worked out on the exercise machine. Connie asked Baum what he thought of Jerry Mack.

"An amiable hack," Baum said. "His award-winning documentaries are all love letters. Nothing hard-hitting or investigative."

"The people he chooses deserve love letters. They're all stars in their fields. I know you don't agree because your standards are so high," Connie said, the final words jam-packed with denigrating sarcasm.

"Let's not start that again. He thinks the world of Thane and his writing and I agree that a feature on TV will sell a lot of books. Nevertheless, you asked me what I thought of him and I think he's pleasant but an airhead."

"I don't think he's happily married," Connie said.

"Really? How do you know that?" Baum asked, suspicion aroused to the max.

"From things he said. How else?"

"My god, he's a stranger and he opened up to you about his unhappy marriage?"

"He didn't open up. We got on the subject of marriage and I kind of picked up on things he said. And I don't find him an airhead. He's actually quite brilliant. Education at Harvard."

"Same as you."

"Yes. He majored in political science and switched to filmmaking." It suddenly became clear as a bell to Baum. Allegedly Mack was surveying the grounds for a shoot but somehow managed to manipulate the conversation to marriage so he could let Connie know he might be available.

"You didn't know each other at Harvard I assume?"

"No. Shame because we share so many nice memories. Even had some of the same teachers."

"Well, he certainly is quite taken with you. And Thane of course."

And now she was crying.

"What? What's wrong?"

"I don't know. I'm just feeling a little blue today."

"Are you still upset because I was critical of Thane's work?"

"No. It's not always about you, Asher."

"I didn't mean it that way."

"I had some wine for lunch. And yes, I was furious with you."

"I apologize."

"And Jerry Mack brought back memories of my days at Harvard. I was happy there."

"I'm sure you were."

"I had my whole life ahead of me," she said and sank into a chair. "So much to look forward to."

Baum stood there seeing her weep. Stood there quietly for a few seconds and then he was crying, blubbering and fumbling for a Kleenex. He put his hand in his pocket and pulled out a huge wad of fresh Kleenex. He raged against a universe where they promised you when you took a Kleenex a fresh one would pop up but whenever the box became half full the Kleenex stopped popping up and he had to grasp them manually and inevitably took fat stacks of them because it was too hard to just take one. This was a betrayal and he raged against it as vehemently as the fate of mankind.

"What the hell are you crying about?" Connie said.

"I don't know," Baum said.

"What do you mean you don't know?"

"I don't know why I'm crying, okay? I'm weeping but I can't exactly give you a specific reason."

"Well Jesus Christ, stop. That loud sobbing is not very manly."

Now Connie rose and stormed off leaving her husband wiping away tears and gradually pulling himself together.

"For god's sake, what are you so torn up about?" he heard himself saying.

"I don't know. You gonna get on me? I'm not in the mood."

"You don't know why you're crying?"

"No."

"Well lighten up."

"I'm okay."

"Can I tell you why you were crying?"

"You know?"

"You were crying because nothing works. The universe, the Kleenex box, your life, your work, your marriage. And I think you're under stress waiting for the other shoe to drop from the little Japanese girl which probably bothers you more than you realize. Everything's unraveling."

"Did I tell you Connie's getting a dog? A Doberman. Same dog Himmler had."

Baum couldn't write that day and that night when he climbed into bed next to Connie he was fatigued. He still had feelings for his wife but he could no longer tell exactly what those feelings were.

Mixed feelings was the best he could come up with. There were many things on his mind and he fought to sort out his bewilderment with consciousness ebbing and oblivion finally taking the trick. The next morning he awoke, at first a little foggy. He zombied his way through breakfast, and with coffee he managed to reboot.

"Where are you this morning?" Connie said.

"I guess I woke up a little hungover, but I'm okay."

"I spoke with Jerry Mack last night and he truly believes Thane has a good chance to win the National Book Award."

"Uh-huh."

"Jesus Christ, did I ruin your day?"

"I wish him luck."

"Jerry told me how you tried to torpedo him. He was shocked."

It's Jerry already, he thought.

"Frankly, he couldn't believe a father would talk about a son like that."

"Stepson."

"Believe me, I know Thane does not have your genes."

"It's early and we're off to a great start," Baum said, hoping to de-escalate.

"Well, it was on my mind all night and I had terrible dreams."

"I'm surprised you didn't wake me to have it out."

"I wanted to."

"You have to watch that temper."

"Yes, I have a temper and I say things I later regret. And you know how to push all the right buttons."

"I had wine on an empty stomach when I criticized Thane. You can rest easy. I'll say nice things only about him on camera. I had trouble sleeping too. Can we put it behind us?"

"Good morning," Sam said entering the room and energizing it. "I know you wanted to leave early. Do I have time for coffee?"

"Sure," Baum said, predictably thinking how pretty she looked, her figure validating her sweater and skirt. Connie gave Sam juice, coffee and a corn muffin.

"Did you sleep well?" Connie asked her.

"Very well. The country air. Thane is still out."

"He needs at least eight hours," Connie said. "Better nine. He's working on an idea for his next novel."

"He looks só handsome lying there, out like a light," Sam said.

"I know that look," Connie said. "Young Alain Delon."

Baum winced without moving his body or facial muscles, a trick he had learned over the years, and waited for Sam to finish her coffee. All those breakfasts with Tyler, her oatmeal with honey and her freshly ground French Roast. He seemed deep in thought, a man with a secret. When Sam finished and rose he left the kitchen and pulled the car onto the edge of the driveway. Sam hurried along and got in. He pulled out and he noticed she became more beautiful when she put on her sunglasses. Earlier he had gotten off in a minor key with Connie, now he was groovin' high with Sam as they drove through the countryside. They made small talk. Yes, the leaves were through with summer and now they were going out in a blaze of red and yellow glory. The war in the Middle East was a true tragedy, "The Emperor of Ice Cream" was one of my favorite poems too, did you ever see a Renoir film called *A Day in the Country?* Fabulous.

"I like driving with you," she said. "You're confident. Thane is always so nervous. He's very high strung. Did you ever notice that?"

It was the first time in his life anyone ever complimented his prowess behind the wheel. Tyler used to tease him because he always got lost. Sam's praise caused him to take even more virile command of the road, press the gas pedal and soon get pulled over for speeding. He got off with a warning from the merciful Connecticut trooper. They had a laugh over it and after that he took it easy.

"I'm glad you're driving in. It's such a bore going alone and Thane is busy writing. We gave him such a big advance. I mean the publisher did."

"I have a meeting with a publisher," Baum said. "I never take an advance. Too much pressure to deliver."

"Which publisher?"

"Do you know Roadhouse?"

"Yes. They're okay. Kind of a renegade operation. Is it with Shivay Banerjee?"

"Yes. Banerjee. He told my ex-agent he wanted to talk to me about my new book."

"You shouldn't waste your time with Roadhouse. They're so small. And Shivay's a little off the wall. Well, you'll see.

You won't get an advance and not much promotion. But you said you don't take an advance—which is smart I think. You should talk to my boss, Henry Cobb. You'd love him. He's Thane's publisher."

"I know but I don't know him."

"I'm surprised Thane never introduced you to Henry. I think he'd like your work. He may have even seen some of it or said something to Thane."

"Thane never mentioned it."

"Must have slipped his mind."

Sure, Baum thought, sure it slipped his mind. Thane would never recommend him to his publisher. Thane had contempt for his writing and more to the point, contempt for him sleeping in the same bed as his mother.

"Maybe because he knows you had a publisher," Sam said. "Henry's the most ethical, decent human being. Ask anyone about his reputation. Anyone."

"I know he's respected, very looked up to."

"He's a dear, sweet man with a temper but his temper is on the side of the angels. You'd love him. I'm surprised Thane didn't bring you two together. He trusts Thane's judgment."

"I had a falling out with my publisher, so I left them. Or should I say, they asked me to leave them."

"Well, you have to meet Henry. I remember he once had some nice things to say about your book to Thane."

"I'd love to meet him," Baum said, beginning to feel a little hope about his prospects.

"Ask her to lunch."

"I was going to." There was Baum talking to Baum.

"What?" Sam said. "Did you say something?"

"Me?"

"Just now."

"I was asking if you were free for lunch."

"I'm free all day. I'd love to have lunch."

"Then it's a date. After our meetings I'll pick you up."

"Just call first. If my meetings run long."

Baum dropped Sam on Madison and Thirty-Third and watched her hurry into her office building.

"What do you expect to happen, Asher?" he said to himself as he pulled off and drove to a parking garage.

"You mean with Roadhouse?"

"Not Roadhouse, boob, Sam. Roadhouse is a business meeting."

"Nothing with Sam. I was just planning to spend some time with her. Lunch if she's free, possibly catch the Pissarro show at the Met if she's up to it, and then back to Connecticut."

"Uh-huh."

"If you think I have anything else on my mind, you're wrong."

"Just don't make any more sudden lunges. Did you check the paper to see if you're in there?"

"The minute I got up. So far nothing. Meanwhile I've got enough on my mind. I have a meeting with a publisher and now Sam says she can set me up with Henry Cobb. Wouldn't that be a coup."

"I agree Henry Cobb is a prestigious house. Roadhouse is okay but nothing by comparison."

"Can you believe Cobb was interested in me and that little bastard Thane never told me? He never brought us together."

"Why does this come as a surprise to you, Asher? You know what he thinks about you. So why would he want to recommend you to his publisher, Cobb, who publishes major authors?"

"Maybe I'll take Sam for lunch at Balthazar. I know Keith and I could call him and get a quick reservation. Nice quiet table in a corner."

"You poor thing."

"What does that mean?"

"You can't relive the past."

"Did I tell you she reminds me of Tyler?"

"Only a thousand times."

Baum pulled into a garage and parked his car for the usual king's ransom, scooted over to the building that housed Roadhouse Publications and decided on the staircase. I'll take my chances with eleven flights and a possible heart attack rather than die stuck between floors in a vertical coffin, he thought.

He arrived at eleven out of breath but still certain he'd made the right choice. He was ushered wheezing into the office of Banerjee. Banerjee was an older, gray-haired, nice-looking man, very well mannered, who apparently saw something in Baum's writing which he felt had not yet come off.

"Clearly you have a talent and clearly you were for some years a journalist," Banerjee said. "You are full of facts, details, editorial points of view instead of human emotions. This is where you fall down. You are so intent on taking on big themes, the ones that answer the unanswerable, you fall over yourself philosophizing. Leave the fate of mankind to the true intellectuals, of which clearly you are not. Your job is to create living, breathing human beings, not vehicles to espouse your cliched ideas or vent your weltschmerz or like Job's wife, curse God, or if there is none, impotently flail at empty space. I get the feeling from your books that though you profess to not like people, you actually care a great deal about them."

"In my heart I feel a huge sadness for my species," Baum said, trying to match Banerjee's lofty *pronunciamientos*. "They act the way they do out of fear and panic and if I could find some redeeming loophole to soothe them and accept their fate if not with joy at least without terror, I would do so."

"This is not your job as an artist. Your job first and foremost is to entertain. Then, if you also have something of value to say, fine. But a message delivered in an unentertaining way is death for the artist."

"But I'm not in show business. I admit my goal may turn out to be too ambitious, but I want to try and change the reader's life."

"But boring him with a book he's just spent twenty-six dollars on only adds to his suffering." Banerjee lit a cigarette. "You are not Dostoevsky," the publisher continued, "though it is clear you would like to be. And even he had great humor. As did Kafka. But why talk about geniuses. You are not one. I'm sure you realize that. I don't mean to imply that you don't have your own limited gift, occasional flashes of wit and imagination. My candid opinion is that you have too much anger and it is another reason your writing becomes dull. Turgid is the word everybody uses when talking about you. By the way I hope I'm not offending you."

"Don't be silly—I love being run through a paper shredder."

"I'm frank with you because there is something in your work worth nurturing. I hate to see it drowned in bile and pedantry."

"Unfortunately bile and pedantry is my strong suit," Baum said rising. "I appreciate your interest in me but I'm double-parked."

"Did you ever think that perhaps unconsciously you wanted your book to have small sales so you can say you have a select public and in some distorted way, tell yourself that makes you an artist?"

"Any other criticism? You haven't said anything about the way I'm dressed."

"I see I have offended you," Banerjee said. "Tell me what is it you're so angry about?"

For a moment Baum's eyes lost focus. "Because I was born without the ability to self-deceive."

"I understand," Banerjee said, nodding. "One of the tools of survival. Still, one must cope."

Baum sat silent, a bit transfixed. "Look," the Indian said, "think about it. If anything I said makes sense to you and you're willing to consider it next time you write, perhaps we can work together. I leave you with this advice: To write a great novel, one must at all costs keep the reader interested in what happens next. If you also want to enrich his mind, to make a statement that is truly wise—go over the book with an editor and take out the wisdom."

Baum left unsettled. He had expected a much different encounter and began to realize that his agent had probably had to talk Banerjee into meeting with him and not because the Indian was champing at the bit. The Roadhouse publisher may have agreed because he did a lot of business with Bell and respected him as an agent. Baum couldn't process what he was getting from Banerjee who had a commanding presence but did nothing to temper his criticism or ingratiate himself. The fact was he was brutal. And yet Banerjee did not come across as a con man or a fool. Perhaps it was the Hindu veneer, calm, sage, profound. What the hell did he mean by that last remark, to take out the wisdom? Baum now considered himself very lucky Sam was setting up a meeting with Henry Cobb who would either publish him or not but would spare him the yoga on his approach to literature. Still, priding himself on his open-mindedness, he vowed to consider what Banerjee had said, painful as it was. Take out the wisdom. What an insight. What an absurd insight. And yet…

But now trumping Baum's thoughts was not advice from an Indian publisher but a nice lunch at Balthazar and maybe an afternoon at the art galleries as he once loved doing with Tyler. Lunch was confirmed for him by Sam, who loved Balthazar, and Baum said he'd be by to pick her up. She was tied up in one meeting after another and would be at least an hour late. She said she spoke to her boss and as soon as he could, he would meet with Baum, hopefully next week. This sent a wave of positive electrolytes through Baum's head.

Now he had time to kill. What a phrase, Baum thought. That's life. You kill time till it kills you. Strolling downtown on this unimaginably beautiful autumn day, he had time to think, to hum "I'm wild again, beguiled again," and enjoy the New York streets. Intruding on his pleasant walk were thoughts about his marriage, Connie, allegations bound to hit the fan, Jerry Mack eyeing Connie. He thought of how nice it was to be able to spend a day in Manhattan with Sam Taylor and relive memories of the woman who taught him what it meant to be in love and who caused him to lose control. He thought about why it had been so hard for him to make the transition from journalism to fiction. Every time he ventured into the world of made-up plots and complex humans, he got lost; lost in the stars, in the reasons for everything, he got lost in time and dark matter. But what could he do about it? Write? Try harder? Write better? But take out the wisdom. He wondered if the gray-haired publisher from India was deep or just an Indian.

Baum loved downtown Manhattan. He walked from Chelsea to the beautiful West Village, adoring every tree-lined block. After a while he found himself wandering into a bookstore. He browsed among his betters, thumbing the Russians, the poets he loved, Eliot, Wallace Stevens, Philip Larkin. Naturally, in one section there was Thane's book on display. Owner has to make his nut, he thought. As for the author's picture on the back cover—not since Truman Capote lay siren-like on his divan was there such a study in self-love by an author waiting to be ravaged by praise. Thane had posed on the grass, white shirt unbuttoned to the navel, tanned chest, tight blue jeans, bare feet, wildflowers framing the tableau and a couple of swans on the pond behind him. Definitely to puke, Baum thought. Still, there he was being sold right alongside Proust and Flaubert.

A small roach-like man with big round glasses picked up a copy of Thane's bestseller.

"You don't want that," Baum said. "I read it. Much over-hyped. Very boring."

"I don't doubt it," the roach man said. "I got the whole scoop on this book. I have a friend, a literature nerd who told me all about it."

I wouldn't talk about nerds if I were you, thought Baum.

"Whoever wrote this book stole it all. I hear it's one of the worst cases of plagiary my friend ever saw."

"Really? What makes you say that?" Baum said amused.

"I'm saying it's plagiarized."

"Yeah, so why hasn't anybody said anything?"

"The original is too obscure. The nineteen fifties. Even then few read it."

"So why doesn't your friend say something?"

"He would have maybe but for a massive stroke."

"He had a stroke?"

"In midtown traffic. He was coming from his AA meeting."

"An alcoholic." Baum was by now humoring the little creature.

"The book is blatant thievery. Stole another man's work."

Baum could see the roach man was quite intense and wondered, could this nonsense have a molecule of reality?

"Are you telling me this is plagiarized, and no one has called him out on it?" Baum had thought the roach man was a street crazy who wandered into a bookstore, but he was clean shaven and respectably dressed.

"Sentences, paragraphs, the whole concept he stole, the idea, the people. My friend, unable to speak, paralyzed, was quite upset over it. He said he never saw anything so disgusting."

"The nerd said this? The literary nerd?"

"Yes, yes, Pinchuck, my friend Pinchuck. He's dead."

"What's the book he stole?"

"Oh, what he plagiarized?"

"Yes, what book? By who?"

"Some obscure thing. A title from the bible. Yes. *Impossible for Man*. That's the title. You know the line from the bible, 'impossible for man, possible for God.' You know that line?"

"I don't. No, I don't. Where can I get a copy of this book? Who's the author?"

"I don't know. It's out of print. You'd have to go to a place that sells out of print books." The roach man held up Thane's novel. "So, you read this and it's no good. Doesn't surprise me because you're reading fraudulent merchandise. It's like buying a piece of furniture that's a Grand Rapids reproduction of a genuine antique. Pinchuck told me he modernized it but stole everything. Pinchuck said practically nobody bought the book years ago when it came out. He said the plot is more relevant today than it was then. Didn't mean anything to the critics or the reading public back in the nineteen fifties, but times change. Publisher's long out of business. Amazing someone can get away with something like that."

"Why haven't you said anything?"

"To open a can of worms? I've got other things on my mind. My firm is moving to Vienna. I'm starting a job in a new country. Much more responsibility. Lucky I speak German."

Outside on the street with a fresh breeze cooling down his face, Baum was googling *Impossible for Man*, which was indeed a book by Harry Eastman. Not much about it. So who was this roach-like nerd who talks of yet another nerd who was an alcoholic that had a stroke, who's dead? Would Thane be so conniving and so brazen as to steal plot, characters, dialogue from a dead writer? Hard to believe. Thane's not stupid. And why has it gone unnoticed? On the other hand, he did say the book is very obscure, and plagiarism happens all the time, Baum believed, and we only know of the ones who are caught.

Baum lit out for the Strand where they had every book since Gutenberg showed up at the patent office. Could it be possible? he wondered. What a turn of events! To unmask this phony genius as a hustler, a fake, a scammer. Somehow, Thane could've come across the book, stolen it, given it a little cosmetic makeover and, according to Pinchuck, the roach man's friend, done a clumsy theft at that. Sure enough the Strand had one single copy of *Impossible for Man* and Baum snatched it up. He would bring it home and go over the two books side by side at leisure, developing an incriminating case if all the roach man said was actually true. But the problem was, he couldn't wait. He had time before meeting with Sam. He was reluctant to buy a copy of Thane's book, *The Beveled Heart*, and fatten the sales by twenty-six dollars, yet impatience forced him to pop for the bestseller.

On a side street in the West Village, he found a townhouse with a stoop, made himself comfortable with both hardbacks and began reading *Impossible for Man* by Harry Eastman and comparing it with Thane's book. He was so rapt he never noticed a man coming down the steps to walk his Afghan, stepping right through him and saying excuse me. He read laser-like for an hour and the more he read the more astonished he became over the enormity of the theft. The roach man was right. It was one of the worst cases of plagiarism one could imagine. And for all Thane's brilliance, it was handled ineptly. The attempt at adding contemporary touches was painfully obvious if you saw the original. The whole grift was based on the assumption that no human would ever know of the existence of this out-of-print dead author's obscure novel. What the crafty schemers never realize is that you may be able to fool the brilliant people, the educated, but the world is full of nerds and roach men and them, you won't fool.

But now it was getting late and he had to pick up Sam. He dumped the books in the trunk of his car, bolted up out of the garage and leaving his car there, grabbed a cab to fetch her. He was in possession of a terrible secret.

"What should I do?"

"Don't ask me," he replied to himself. "Takes a little thought."

The cabdriver asked if he was talking to him. He said no and the driver shrugged and drove on. She was there waiting in the curved arch of her office building's entrance, waiting for him with a great smile on her great face which cheered him up no end. The cab ride to Balthazar was a smorgasbord of small talk.

"How'd your meeting go?" she asked.

"He's quite a character, that Indian."

"To say the least. I spoke to Henry Cobb about you. He wants to meet you next week."

"I'm very thankful and anxious to meet with him."

"Isn't today beautiful?" she said. "My horoscope said today would be a special day. I don't believe in it, but I read it every day. 'Autumn in New York,'" she said, "I'm sure you know that pretty song."

"Clifford Brown. Ever hear his recording of it?"

"No," she said.

"You'd love it."

"Tell me about your meeting with Shivay."

"I'm still recovering from it."

"You look all shaken up. Are you okay?"

"I'll tell you over french fries."

What he would tell her was that his meeting with Banerjee had been disturbing and left him a bit shaken up. That people had told him many of the same things before but hearing them from an Indian resonated more.

"Yes," Sam said. "He's a total triumph of style."

What he would not tell her was what he had learned about Thane's book. He wanted so much to share the information with her but he could not bring himself to. This will come as a nasty shock, he thought, and my god, what about Connie? Or does Connie know? Could she be in on it? A mother-son conspiracy. But that's not Connie. She's going to be knocked for a loop. A crushing loop. But could she be aware and just be looking the other way? No, mustn't get carried away. So far nobody's said anything, and very possibly nobody will. If this gets out it will destroy Thane. Goodbye career. To paraphrase a certain Danish prince, it is not nor it cannot come to good but break Sam and Connie's heart so I must hold my tongue.

"Must I hold my tongue?" he said out loud.

"Did you say something?" Sam said.

"Me?" he said, embarrassed.

"Yes. Didn't you mumble something?"

"I was just trying to remember a line from *Hamlet*, 'Rest in reason, move in passion.'"

"I don't think that's Shakespeare."

"No, I guess not but I was thinking that one's brain is not in the head but in the blood."

"I love the way you sink so deep in thought, you talk to yourself," Sam said.

"Did you ever read *Impossible for Man*, a novel by Harry Eastman?"

She thought a moment. "No. *Impossible for Man*? No. Why? Is it great?"

"No, no. It's an old novel. I just happened to remember it."

"What's it about?"

"Oh, just some people who try to change their lives and they wind up changing them for the worse."

"Uh-huh. No. I never heard of it."

Now Baum wanted to get off the subject. He was very uncertain of his feelings. He needed time to be alone. To have some peace and quiet and lay out all his options. To plan how he should handle this damning information. This was not the moment. He had lucked out into a day in the city with a sweet and lovely creature who took him back to the happiest, most intensely lived days of his life and here she was, smiling at him in a cab aimed at Balthazar. Truly a journey into the past.

"I'm so grateful to you for setting up a meeting with Henry Cobb. I really had mixed feelings about Shivay Banerjee."

"I wasn't sure you'd take to him but I didn't want to say anything. It's none of my business. He's very taken with himself. But not stupid. I think you and Henry will hit it off. You're both uncompromising guys. He's very intense, very proper, very moral and high-strung, cares about everything. Lives on pills but if you had to be on a life raft with someone, he's the one. A terrific human being."

Sam clearly thought the world of her boss and felt strongly enough about Baum's work that she brokered a meeting. There was no question Baum had a crush on Sam and while his logic told him it could lead nowhere at best and disaster at worst, the undertow was hard to swim against. He found himself holding every sentence she said under a microscope. The choice of words, the context, the inflection. Do they reveal anything about her inner feelings? There was a silence and then she said, "The plot of that book you mentioned sounds similar to Thane's book."

"Ah look, we're here," he said, mercifully saving him from following up on her observation. After five minutes of gab in Balthazar on great Parisian brasseries they were ordering salads and of course the burgers and fries. The waiter, the snake in this Soho Eden, suggested wine. Sam asked, should they? But fearing that Hysterical Asher would be set free, he said no thank you. She, however, took a bite of the apple and ordered a little Cabernet Sauvignon with her lunch and it wasn't long before she tippled her way into looser charm.

"There seems to be something on your mind," she said. "Are you okay?"

"I'm fine," Baum said. He wanted to say, "You're very sharp. With your intelligence and perception what are you doing with Thane?"

He really was tempted to spill the beans and had he not passed on the Cabernet Sauvignon, he might well have.

"I can tell you're excited to be in New York," she said. "You're like a different person."

"In what way?"

"More up."

"I'm definitely a city mouse. London, Rome, Paris. I like the action."

"And yet, you live in Connecticut amongst bee hives and bird nests."

"Connie couldn't live anyplace else. She can't handle the streets. I grew up in the streets."

"Connie's great, but can I say something about your wife?"

"I know what you're going to say."

"She and Thane are awfully close."

"Tell me about it."

"I mean it's nice in a way how much they admire each other."

"Yes, although some have suggested there's a slightly creepy quality to it."

"No. Don't say that. It's just rare to see such mother-son closeness."

"Connie is convinced she's given birth to a genius."

"Yes, he's a genius. A spoiled genius. Overconfident but when you're as bright as he. I guess I was spoiled too."

Baum noted she didn't say, you also are a genius, just undiscovered.

"Where did you grow up?" he asked her.

"San Francisco. Pacific Heights. My dad was a civil engineer and my mother taught philosophy. They spoiled me. I never heard the word no."

"Like Tyler. You're so much like my ex-wife. You look like her. You say the same things. She was very preceptive too. Especially about my writing. And she was beautiful—like you."

"So, you're a sucker for a pretty face."

Baum had snuck in that compliment to test the waters and see how she'd react but it failed to provide any usable intelligence.

"Connie is a workout," he said, hoping to very subtly imply that perhaps all was not perfect between him and his wife.

"You must love her a great deal to sacrifice your passion for New York City. I know what you think of country life."

"Yes. I suffer from hay fever. And yet I spend my life amongst timothy and ragweed. To atone for my sins."

"What are your sins?"

"What are yours?"

"Sweets. Impatience. What else? Falling for the wrong men."

Bingo, thought Baum, a rich strike.

"And you?" she said.

"My biggest sin is fear."

"And what are you afraid of?"

"Loneliness, black holes, time, burglars, tumors, failure, elevators—I could go on but we'd be here all day."

She smiled and looked at Baum.

"I see. Fear is where those sporadic flashes of inspiration in your work come from. In your own way you're an original."

"An original what?"

"Headcase."

"Thank you, this has been my day for frank appraisals."

"Thane told me about your issues—you've paid some dues but it hasn't made you bitter—angry maybe but you're likable."

"A likable head case."

"And you're so damn interesting. At least to me."

"Did he tell you when Tyler dumped me I had a kind of nervous breakdown?"

"What do you mean, kind of?"

"You're right—it was not kind of, it was a breakdown. My friends thought I was going to harm myself. They checked me into a kind of sanitarium—okay, an actual sanitarium. And then I was walking down this long hall to the room they were putting me in, I don't know why because they had no intention of it, but I got the mistaken notion they were going to give me shock therapy and knock me out with electricity, so I panicked and made a run for it, but they stopped me and gave me some stuff that eventually calmed me down."

"How long were you in for?"

"Just a few days. Maybe a week or two. So, you're right in saying I'm a headcase but that was some time ago, although lately I've had some of the same kind of anxieties. Like I'm losing it. It's hard to explain."

"I know a critic said you whine but I find something universal in your whining. I know I'm in the minority."

"I appreciate you introducing me to Henry Cobb."

"So you really were in love with Tyler, your ex."

"It's amazing how much you remind me of her. Did I say that? You look like her and here I am sitting with you in Balthazar."

"Is that why you wanted to spend time with me? Because I remind you of Tyler?"

"Probably," he said, enjoying all the flirtatious drivel between them but knowing he could not and would not act on it.

"Well then let's at least enjoy the day," she said. "Shall we hit the streets and see some art?"

"I'll get a check. I hope it's a big one to punish me for my guilt over this conversation." Still flirting, he took care of business and they left.

They worked Soho and the Meatpacking District. Some of the art was wonderful and some was not so wonderful. Baum loved art and thought of all the young artists struggling to emerge in a world that loved art, was moved by art, needed art, and paradoxically gave artists such a hard time. He thought of Thane and a feeling of anger came over him which he filed for later consideration not to spoil his afternoon. They lucked out at a photography exhibit and saw some fabulous Lee Friedlanders and then a few Weegees. They both loved the men's work. They stopped in at the Morgan Library to see some original *Alice in Wonderland* illustrations and she bought an Alice tote bag for her niece.

It reminded Baum of a funny story he told her of when he and Tyler had visited Europe and while in Munich, at his urging they drove out to Dachau, the former Nazi concentration camp that was kept intact and was open to tourists. Both he and Tyler were surprised to find the horrific camp nestled in the beautiful country woods amidst trees and flowers. And there it was, a short drive from town, exactly as seen in the ghastly photos and newsreel footage with its gas chamber and crematorium. There were lovely, manicured spots where prisoners were beaten to death. Thousands of innocent human beings were starved and tortured and threw themselves on the electrical wires to die when it became intolerable. It was as close to hell as one could imagine. On the way out they heard a lady tourist innocently ask at the front desk if there was a gift shop. Sam laughed as hard as he and Tyler had when it happened. They cabbed uptown to the Met and saw the Pissarros. They both had always been tremendous fans of "The Boulevard Montmartre on a Winter Morning." Asher explained how he would love to step into that painting and be there, then, not here, now. Sam laughed and said, take me with you. Later, outside, walking in Central Park, the effect of the picture stayed with him and so did her remark.

"I used to come here with Tyler and stare at the pictures, only she wanted to step into a Renoir. She and I talked a lot about moving to Paris."

"Is that your dream? To live in Paris? It's certainly mine."

"Yes. But the painting is so seductive because it makes you want to be there that specific winter morning. You have to realize, so much of the dream is that you're looking at them in those clothes and in horse and carriages. Imagine dining at Maxime's. Naturally, if I was in that time and place by now I'd be dead. And of course the dentists had no Novocain."

"Yes, life teases, doesn't it?" Sam said. "So much charm and beauty, so much Dachau."

"If you're lucky you wind up with a rock on a hill. What good is a rock on a hill? It's nothing. It's nothing. I'm sorry I didn't mean to rant so loud."

"What if it's not a rock but a great book?"

"You're very perceptive but ask me that question in a few billion years when to paraphrase Gertrude Stein, there's no here here."

"You bring pessimism to new heights. And I was just going to say how divine it must've been living in Paris in the belle epoque. To live in a Renoir painting."

"Of course, the people you see in the Renoir painting probably longed to live in the Fragonards."

As they strolled in the park parallel to Fifth Avenue and chatted, the warm lights of New York apartments started going on making the tableau through the foliage very romantic and Samantha Taylor became more and more beautiful as dusk stole in.

It was the nicest time he'd had in a long time but of course would end badly as there was nowhere to go with it despite the fact she found him "likable" and "so damn interesting." He was a "headcase" but his whining was "universal." Oh well. This day would be a throwback to sweeter years, and he felt lucky to get it in while he could still do fifteen push-ups.

Then, an amazing thing happened. Something out of a movie or a dream, not the usual fare from life's routine theatrical season of flops. They decided to leave the park and walk to his parked car. They were heading down Fifth laughing over some trivial thing because one thing that made the day fun was that they laughed at many of the same things, some grave, some foolish. They decided to have one quick drink at the Bemelmans Bar before driving back to Connecticut because both he and she loved that bar with the artist's fabulous murals. Sam had an actual original Bemelmans watercolor of Madeline, a gift from her parents. Plus, they had been talking about Paris so lovingly the past half hour. And so they turned off the avenue and headed across Seventy-Seventh to The Carlyle hotel and reaching Madison Avenue, who do he and Sam run smack into but Tyler. Tyler? Yes, it was Tyler Royce, once Tyler Baum, now Tyler Lake. Sam knew who she was right off, not so much from Baum's description of her looks, but from his physical reaction, which was probably comparable to when the meteor wiped out the dinosaurs. Baum stood there stupefied.

"Hi Asher," she said bubbling over with a bright smile. "What a nice surprise."

Baum, frozen like the victim of blunt force trauma, stood there, and the only word in the English language he could think of was, "Tyler." Then, the neurons in his brain started firing and he came up with, "What are you doing here?" My god, he thought, I can do better than that. He was failing this Noel Coward moment.

"Ricky's friend is getting married so we're here for his wedding. You look good."

"So do you," was all he could think of. What's wrong with me? I usually have such a flair for dialogue.

She hadn't aged much and where she had it was commensurate with her natural beauty. No Botox here sabotaging that wonderful farm-to-table face. She looked sparkling, healthy, beautiful. Apparently, tending sheep agreed with her. Of all the things they had been through together, only that first moment, standing by her doorbell, talking to her over the intercom came back most vividly, most poignantly. All that was missing from this chance encounter was a full orchestra scoring the moment.

"This is Sam," he said having finally achieved maximum awkwardness. "She's my stepson's girlfriend."

"Then what are you doing with her?" Tyler said and laughed though Baum turned red.

And then the women acknowledged one another warmly and for a moment he was seeing a double feature, the original and the sequel.

"How's your work coming?" Tyler asked. "I read your book. If I had more time, I'd love to talk to you about it but we're making a plane tonight. Twenty-seven hours in the air. Just your thing," she said sarcastically.

"I'm sure you're anxious to get back home. The sheep need tending." Baum's hurt was returning, his mixed emotions.

"It's definitely not for you." Tyler said. "'All animals are failed humans,' I remember you once saying."

"Oh, sheep are different, I could never resist a good wool shearing. Or watching the fold graze in a meadow, a Collie by my side. Or for that matter a couple of lamb chops with mint jelly."

"Stop with the bullshit, Asher. It happens to be very fulfilling. And educational. I'll bet you don't know the pupils in the eyes of sheep are rectangular."

"I didn't, although how I managed so many years on Manhattan's Upper East Side without knowing that fact. Just goes to show you."

"Actually, you'd like sheep. You have something in common with them. They self-medicate."

"What does that mean?"

"Like you, they eat certain plants not for food but to combat disease and they know which ones cure them."

Baum never thought that when he first met and fell in love with Tyler Royce, a sophisticated die-hard New Yorker who frequented opening nights and trendy restaurants, that years later he'd be standing on Madison Avenue with her, now his ex-wife, discussing her life in New Zealand. When the poet Robert Burns wrote "the best-laid plans of mice and men gang aft a-gley" he didn't know how goddamned a-gley they could actually gang.

"We were just going for a drink. Would you like to join us?" Sam said.

"I'd love to but I can't. But thanks anyway. I'm late already but it was great seeing you, Ash."

"Yes. You too. Otherwise, I would never have known sheep's eyes have rectangular pupils."

And with a smile, she split, walking up Madison Avenue to whatever came next in the adventures of Tyler Royce, Park Avenue Shepherdess.

Despite what he might have told Sam, he was shaken up by the moment with his ex and after he and Sam sat down in the Bemelmans Bar, when she ordered a margarita, he ordered one too.

"I thought you hated hard alcohol," Sam said.

"I do. I really hate the taste of it. I'm just going to sip mine. This really took me by surprise. But I have to drive home."

"She really rattled you."

"I'm okay," he lied, a little embarrassed. "I should have known sheep have rectangular pupils. Where's my drink?"

"I can hear your heart beating from here," she said.

Baum excused himself. "I need to slap some cold water on my face. If I'm not back in five minutes call New York Hospital."

For Baum this had been an unreal encounter, and he wanted a moment's breathing space. He was completely surprised and taken aback he had run into Tyler after all that went on, causing a flood of impressions, the walks, the talks, the laughs, her lips, her jokes, her spaghetti. Suddenly, as Larry Hart so perfectly put it, it had been orange juice for one. He recalled someone mentioning a straitjacket, but it never quite got to that. "We have no intention of giving you ECT, Mr. Baum. Where did you get that idea?"

Ironically, I was the opposite of violent, he remembered. They weren't sure.

"You were a bit out of control," they said.

"I was fine till I heard the words Electric Convulsive Therapy."

"You misunderstood, Mr. Baum. You may have heard it somewhere but never in connection with you. Calm down."

And now he was alone in the restroom of The Carlyle hotel. There he spoke up. "Hey, did you see what just happened?"

"How could I miss it?"

"She looked good."

"Tyler? Yeah, she's got the kind of looks that age well."

"And she still has that sexy vibe. Guys were always hitting on her."

"Yeah, but she was pretty settled with me. Till she wasn't. Or at least I thought so. This guy in New Zealand—she's lasted with him a long time now. New Zealand. What the hell is she doing in New Zealand?"

"Don't wrack your brain because you'll never understand. You said it yourself. Not everything in life can be understood. She's a girl who prefers mutton to midtown."

"Spare me the wit."

"And there were no red flags?"

"None. I try to think what I did wrong."

"Well, that's life. Life is not an exact science."

"Did you see, she still has that great overbite? I forgot how crazy I got over that overbite. Sam has an overbite. And just as sexy as Tyler's. Sam's got a great pout. Tyler has the best pout I ever saw. Listen to me, I'm drowning in pouts and overbites."

"You're unraveling, Asher. You've been on a downslide for a long time now."

"When I first met Tyler she had a silver retainer. I don't know if I ever told you that. So seductive. Christ, why should a retainer turn me on? A lousy piece of metal. Sam has no retainer but she'd look good with one."

"Asher, you're not listening to me. I'm saying you've got to get a grip on yourself."

Baum at that point seemed to ignore all suggestions he was falling apart.

"I was having such a wonderful time with Sam when Tyler showed up. It was so beautiful—like seeing two moons. Isn't there a second small moon they discovered?"

"The resemblance is striking. When I saw the two of them together and you in the middle it was surreal."

"Today was like spending a day with Tyler. Balthazar, the galleries, Central Park, and then the real Tyler. I can't get my mind around this."

"Me neither."

"It's all too much. Sam, Tyler, the roach in the bookstore. So Thane, that little fake, stole everything. I knew it. Didn't I say he was a phony? Didn't I?"

"You did."

"You said no."

"I admit I was skeptical."

"Did you read this guy's book? Harry Eastman? Thane stole some of it word for word."

"Have you decided what you're going to do about it?"

"I don't know. I need a drink. Didn't I order a drink? Where the hell's my margarita?"

"I wouldn't. You know what happens to you with just wine."

"I'm sorry, I need a drink. I need something to settle me."

At that moment the door to the restroom opened, a small man was about to come in, saw Baum ranting to thin air, quickly shut the door and went away.

"You're scaring people. You talking to yourself is getting out of hand."

"You should talk. And it wasn't that," Baum said. "He was one of those poor sensitive souls that can't use a restroom unless it's totally empty. People are crazy with their bathroom issues. We're defective creatures. In heaven, when God created man, he rushed to get the job done in six days. Where was the fire? He wanted that seventh day off to do what? Nap in the fucking clouds? What the hell decent can you make in six days? Especially something as complicated as people."

Baum was babbling off the deep end, taking stage in the bathroom's tile theater.

"And another thing, just before we're sent to earth to be born, some angel takes a little wind-up ratchet timer and gives it a twist and inserts it in your body and depending on the strength of his twist, that's how long you get. It's a timer. The angel usually twists it up in the eighties and then sticks it in you. Some get a stronger twist, or if you're unlucky you could get a short twist. The timer starts clicking, and when that timer stops you shut off. It's all a given. It doesn't matter how much treadmill you do, how much omega-3 you swallow. It's all in that little wind-up timer the angel sticks in you at birth."

By now, Baum was breathing heavy and really needed his margarita. He wanted to see Sam, sit opposite her like he used to sit across from Tyler, and get well from tequila. He wanted to feel happy and sad at the same time. Why sad? Because there was pleasure in sadness too. Why? Because nothing makes sense. He was right, many things in life could not be explained. Sam was waiting at the table, lit from a warm lamp with a pink glow, immensely flattering. She was into her second margarita. He moved into his seat, treated himself to a good look at her. His margarita was waiting.

"You have to be careful," he said, watching her drink. "You don't want too much salt. Not good for the blood pressure...."

A Jewish hypochondriac to the core. Here is a beautiful woman in a dim café over cocktails and suddenly he's worried about the salt around the rim of the glass being bad for her blood pressure.

"You were gone a long time," she said. "Are you okay?"

"Yes. What did you think of Tyler?"

"As you described her. Very lovely. I'm sure she's as amazing as you say she was."

You are also amazing, thought Baum and instead of his usual adagio sipping of any beverage with more than 12 percent alcohol, he folded his hand around his margarita and knocked it back like the lead in a cowboy movie. There he sat smiling, rubicund, every blood vessel in his head dilated to the max. Sam was also feeling the effects of her second round. The two sat looking at one another in the late afternoon silence of the bar, music by the cocktail pianist, a Vernon Duke tune, color by technicolor. If ever there was, as chess players say, a move just crying out to be played, here it was. And much as he would have liked to have opened, something kept him from pushing his pawn to K-4. And so it was finally Sam who took his hand.

"I had a wonderful time today," she said.

"Yes, it was great fun," he said, stunned by her boldness.

"Can I tell you something? Something I've wanted to tell you. Unless you already know it."

Cue the dopamine, and the camera dollies in for a closeup. Baum thought, If it's any version of, in the short time

I've known you, Asher, I've grown very fond of you, he hoped he would not hear it, although he longed to hear precisely those words. One road led to bliss, one road led to hell. The problem was, the road to bliss was really the long way around to hell.

The fact is he really didn't know what he wanted. He just knew he had once been to hell and did not want a return visit. Still, he already smelled some burning sulfur. He thought he would wait till she spoke and then observe his own body and see what it did. He'd clock himself from a distance and as a mere onlooker might not then be responsible for any action his persona would attempt. He wondered if he'd fall victim to Bad Asher or would Good Asher muscle out that gargoyle version of himself and slip back into the world of common sense? What would Kant do if she took his hand? Kant would fall back on the categorical imperative. He would reason, What if all people acted like that, like Bad Asher? Or would Kant, if she took his hand, take her to a hotel room where they could be alone and then write two thousand opaque pages, impossible to understand, justifying it?

"Can I tell you about Thane?" she said.

He thought, Here it comes and what do I do? It will be some version of, I don't know how to break it to Thane, but I've developed a crush on you. Asher couldn't wait to see how Asher would react.

Sam fixed him with her large sensual eyes and said, "Thane asked me to marry him and I'm very excited about it. Connie is the only one he's told and she's over the moon. She had her heart set on Thane and me getting serious and now it's happened. I admit I was trepidatious at first. I think Thane is a tremendous writer and in the past I've always had trouble falling for the artist and not the man. I spent a lot of nights crying. But Thane is not just an artist. He's a fine human being. He has integrity and compassion and I talked it over with my shrink at great length and I'm committed. The reason I'm telling you this is because I know you and Thane have never hit it off and you never managed to get close. I was hoping now that I'm coming into the family, so to speak, and you and I spoke the same language, that I might be able to bring you two together, something Connie has never been able to do. So that's what I wanted to bring up and I thought after a nice day this would be a good time. Have I overstepped my boundaries? You can tell me."

Baum sat there staring not at Sam, not into the middle distance, but into eternity. He didn't know what to say; he didn't know what he thought. He was lost, both in the cosmos and at the Bemelmans Bar.

"Uh-huh," he muttered. He remained silent. He breathed in and out slowly, swallowing immense disappointment. Finally, he spoke. "Did you ever read *Impossible for Man?*" he said, the margarita having worked its prestidigitation.

"No, you asked me that," Sam said. "It's a novel, right?"

"It's an old novel from the last century. Harry Eastman. Name mean anything to you?"

"No."

"I came across it by chance. The author's dead."

"I don't know it. Did you hear what I just said about you and Thane and me being a kind of peacemaker?"

"I realize you didn't read it. Few people have."

"I never heard of *Impossible for Man*. Why? Am I in for a treat if I read it?"

"A treat? No, no. I predict that if you read that book you will think twice about marrying Thane." This was the first heavy-handed thing he had said, and he regretted it as soon as it slipped out. Too dramatic an opening and now, inside his brain, chaos, the dance of the infidels.

"What are you talking about, Asher?" she said. "Are you drunk already?"

"Thane stole practically his whole book from *Impossible for Man*. It's one of the worst, most blatant plagiarisms I've ever seen."

"I don't know what you're talking about, Asher. I think you're drunk."

"Part of me says I should shut up and keep my mouth closed and maybe it will pass unnoticed but whether it does or doesn't, I have to alert you."

"Alert me about what? What are you talking about?"

"It was pointed out to me today that Thane plagiarized his book."

Woody Allen

"That's crazy. By who?"

"The roach man told me about it in a bookstore today. But it is such an egregious theft of another man's work and part of me says I should give it to a journalist and let one of them blow this sleazy crime wide open. That I owe it to my fellow writers, to all the real writers struggling and trying to write an honest book. That I owe it to the legacy of the dead author and to the culture at large. Also to your boss, Mr. Cobb, who is in for an awful embarrassment for publishing it. One thing I do know however, now that you've told me you're thinking of marrying him and in the past you've sometimes confused the artist with the man and since in this case Thane is neither an artist nor an honest man, I felt obliged to try and save you from walking off a cliff."

And now, all was quiet at the Bemelmans Bar except for the cocktail pianist going into "Moonglow." The happy hour crowd had just started filtering in with a slight buzz but right now enough silence still prevailed.

"I don't believe you," Sam finally said but there was no question Baum had shaken her slightly.

"I'm assuming of course that this is information you didn't know and go along with."

"I don't believe you," she said, and whether it was the color change in her cheeks or the moisture gathering in her eyes, it was clear she was not taking it well.

"I wouldn't lie," Baum said. "I'm thinking of your future."

"No one is saying you're lying," she said, more than the barest tinge of testiness creeping into her delivery. "I'm saying you're a little drunk and you've had a traumatic encounter with your ex and you're a bit rattled."

"I'm okay Sam, and yes, seeing Tyler threw me and one margarita is more than I can handle but I'm probably somewhat drunk and maybe I shouldn't have said anything, but I thought you should hear it now."

"Connie always says you're very competitive with Thane and resent his success. Obviously, you've been writing far longer and have never really published anything that has connected as deeply with the public as Thane's first try."

"No, I'm not very commercial but you always knew that."

"You haven't been critically accepted. No one's saying you don't have talent or denying there's potential there but as the years go by one wants to see some of that potential realized." She was tearing up, feeling her second margarita as he felt his first. "Connie says you're bitter because the promise you showed has been unfulfilled. So far. I'm only saying so far. That's why I think if you work with Henry Cobb he may be able to help you and you will turn out that work of art that has eluded you all this time. Or Shivay Banerjee if you can stomach him. That's all I'm saying, and I've only had two drinks to your one." She had ranted her way off the nitty-gritty of what Baum had thrown her way and he was now in for a penny.

"He stole it, Sam. Not just the plot but the characters, sometimes speeches or paragraphs so close, verbatim in some cases."

"Do you know what you're saying? Plagiarism is a crime. But the crime is the least of it. If I thought what you're saying about Thane was true—or are you trying to assassinate his character?" She was clearly scrambled now, refusing to buy there was any chance in the universe that there was a scintilla of truth to this absurdity.

"I'm aware plagiarism is a crime," Baum said. "From the Latin *plagium*. Kidnapping, literary theft. Don't you think I know my Latin?"

"I respect you, Asher. I also know lately you've been under great stress and you've started talking to yourself. Your recent work hasn't gone well, the play that you worked on for a year was very poorly received. Perhaps too harshly reviewed but still it must've hurt. Then you got lectured by that Indian fakir Shivay Banerjee, you run into a woman who broke your heart, you should have seen the look on your face. She brought back memories of a breakdown, and you tell me this story about a roach-like man in a bookstore who tells you about some obscure book."

"I'm going to give you the book."

"And then you tell me the man I love and decided to marry is a fraud who's been deceiving me. He's not the man I should marry because I'm walking off a cliff." She was weeping now, voice breaking up and rising. "Excuse me," she said and went off to the ladies room leaving Baum sitting alone, talking to himself at a small round table in a dark corner of the Bemelmans Bar, a black silhouette against a mural of Madeline in Paris.

"You happy? Now that you sent her off in tears?"

"What am I supposed to do, let her marry that fraud and find out when it's too late?"

"Maybe she'd never find out. Maybe nobody'd ever find out. Nobody has yet. Maybe it will pass unnoticed if you don't get on your high horse over this literary theft as you keep calling it and blow the whistle."

"I didn't blow any whistle. I know a half dozen guys who would kill to get this story. You don't see me calling any of them. But she's walking into a bad situation, and I can stop her or at least warn her about a terrible mistake, so I should keep quiet? Let her find out the hard way? Even if it never came out, so what happens when he writes his next book? Who does he steal that one from? I mean what kind of guy would even do such a thing?"

At that point a waiter came over and very diplomatically asked him if he could tone it down; that the nearby tables were being bothered. Baum glanced around and saw the place had started to get its first after-work patrons, and he got the once-over from a few customers.

"Oh, excuse me," Baum said, "I didn't realize." As soon as the waiter left, Baum whispered, "Christ, can you keep it down?"

"I was just saying, it's not your responsibility to expose him. I'm not saying he doesn't deserve it, but let somebody else do it."

"Yes, yes, I know what you're going to say. Shut up and walk away."

"It's a miracle nobody's come out so far to accuse him of plagiarism. But whether he's caught or not is not the issue. What does it say about Thane? She should marry a guy capable of such calculated deceit?"

"I feel sorry for him. You get some idea of how insecure and how all that external bravado is because he's desperate."

"Desperate for what?"

"For his mother's approval. What are you, thick? To live up to her image of him as something special."

"But if she marries him and then her husband is unmasked as a disgrace. What then for poor Sam?"

"You'll call me a cliché expert but I say let sleeping dogs lie. Let life take its course without your righteous interference. Don't save the girl. Don't save all the struggling honest writers. Don't save humanity from the hostile cosmos. Butt out."

Beautiful Sam returned to the table. More composed now, she sat and said, "Do you have a copy of the book over which this alleged crime occurred?"

Her voice had grown colder. The lovely day was now history. Even the weather had changed outside but he didn't know it. Baum shifted in his chair, then said, "In the trunk of my car. Along with a copy of Thane's book. I needed both to compare."

"I understand. May I borrow it? Thane's book I have."

"Yes, sure. Sam, I hope—"

She cut him off. "I believe you mean well, Asher. But this is serious stuff. It affects other people's lives. Mine, Thane's and of course, Connie, Henry Cobb who had such a joy in discovering Thane."

Baum could not listen to this litany of consequences without regretting he opened his big mouth. A wave of rage passed over him toward fate for allowing him and the roach man to show up at the bookstore at the same exact moment. But then he and Tyler showed up at the same deli at the same moment. Luck, chance, fate. Who can live in such a world and stay sane?

"What did I do, Sam? What did I do? I only meant to alert you to a terrible situation."

"Okay. I understand. Now give me the book. I'm not going to go back to Connecticut with you. I'd like to go over the book to see for myself. I'll sleep at my own apartment tonight. After I've had some food in my stomach and some coffee, I'll check out what you're saying very carefully before I run off half-cocked which is one of my worst traits."

"Can I buy you dinner?"

"That won't be necessary. I have stuff at home."

Oh god, Asher thought. She hates me. I meant to do a good thing. She even admitted I meant to do a good thing but now she gives off an icy vibe.

"Come," he said, "we'll go to my car and I'll get you the book. And then I'll drive you home."

"Fine."

Fine, he thought. A cold monosyllable. She rose to leave, and as he rose, he said to himself. "Well, what did you expect?"

"What?" she said, not catching it as she was already a step ahead of him going out.

"Nothing, nothing. I was just going to say I know you're upset and I apologize for being the one bearing the bad news. Don't kill the messenger." No answer. Even less than a monosyllabic response. Oy, what did I do? I'm worried about her life but I'm the one in free fall.

They walked the few blocks to the garage in silence. It was raining steadily.

In the car neither spoke. Baum switched on the classical music station. Richard Strauss. *Death and Transfiguration*. Perfect. He switched it off when she made a face. Only once did she speak as he threaded through the traffic to her Bank Street address.

"Are you sober enough to make it to Connecticut?" she asked.

"Yes. Why, am I lurching?"

"No, but it's two hours and it's already dark and starting to really come down."

"No, I'm okay."

"This is the end of Thane," she said.

"Maybe not. Maybe I jumped to a conclusion."

"Right," she said bitterly. They stopped in front of a brownstone of which she had the entire second floor. He got the book from the trunk and handed it to her. She paused, gave the cover a moment's glance. He walked her to her door. They were getting wet, the least of it.

"Thank you for today," she said.

"Will you call me when you've read it?"

"If I don't jump out the window."

"You live on the second floor. How much damage can you do?" he said, still trying to lighten the poured-concrete atmosphere. He took her by the shoulders, the same gesture that got him into trouble with the Asian journalist though he did not kiss Sam.

"Look," he said, "we can both forget this ever happened and move on. Could be no one will ever know."

"If what you say is so, I think there are those of us who cannot just move on." With that she turned and climbed her front steps and went in. Soon Baum was heading back to the ticks and turtles. He drove home through increasing rain, forcing him to lean forward to get some vision through the flooded windshield. His back hurt from leaning in so intently. It brought back a memory of many years ago. Why do rainy nights bring back memories? he wondered. Even rainy afternoons. What the hell could it be? What possible connection could there be between 100 percent humidity and the hippocampus? And yet, the drops fall and moments past come rushing back. At least to Baum they always did and as he drove back to Bridgewater, he remembered driving back from a play he had written, the first play he had ever had produced. It had been put on in Provincetown. It had not gone well, and while he had tried his hand at playwriting, he preferred the novel. The play had been a domestic drama about a Bronx family and his mother and father and Ruth Kahn, his then-sweetheart and her parents came as did many friends and it started as a great night. The problem set in when the families and friends began to realize that the characters in the play had been modeled after them, some duplicated in detail. Conflicts, psychological vulnerabilities, foibles and failures abounded alongside the lustful desires and adulterous confidences all up there on the stage for everyone to see. His friend Blitzstein was exposed as a voyeur and David Rosen as a card cheat while his girlfriend's mother came across unmistakably like a harsh virago. His own parents had their share of regrets they would rather not have shared with the public.

Of course, the names had been changed but not even that was very disguised. Helen was Ellen and Jerry, Gerald. But he wrote the play in his youth and while it occurred to him there might be some objections, he thought everything would be taken with good humor which it was not. Baum recalled the ride home, also in a downpour. He drove, his girlfriend next to him and his parents in the back silently fuming. Once, at a red light while he waited for it to change, his father swatted him in the back of the head with a rolled-up program. After that night his girlfriend never spoke to him again. The play was a disaster for other reasons, among them, too many characters, no depth, unintended laughter, but what the hell, he wrote better and even much better as the years passed. Still never quite as good as his nonfiction.

He couldn't avoid getting disproportionally soaked going the short distance from the car to the house. A drowned rat in twenty seconds.

Connie was sitting on the sofa with a drink watching TV. Baum noticed that lately Connie drank more, also starting earlier. Suddenly everybody drinks, he thought. The years have made us drinkers whereas at one time it was a little red or white wine, a beer. Now things seemed to require higher proofs.

"How'd it go?" she said without looking up.

"Okay." He removed his shoes and started to undo his wet ensemble.

"Thane is sick. Nothing serious. We did the COVID test and it's not that. Just a touch of fever. Of course, with him, his baseline is ninety-seven point four and any fraction over it's like a truck hit him."

Poor boy, Baum thought. I'm surprised she doesn't get him into the ICU at Mount Sinai.

"He took two Tylenol and went to bed."

"I'm sure he'll pull through," Baum mumbled.

Meanwhile, he thought, I've got other fish to fry and I'm exhausted from the day's emotional olympics.

"Any calls for me?" he asked.

"No. Didn't Sam come back?"

"She has some business in the city tomorrow."

"Asher," Connie said with breathless relish, "she's going to marry Thane. I'm so excited."

"She is?"

"You might be a little happy for him. He's very excited and she's thrilled. And it's not just a great catch for both of them. He's getting a fabulous young woman. She's exactly the kind of woman he needs to have behind him for a career in literature. She's beautiful and charming and it doesn't hurt that she's moving up in publishing." Connie took another hit of her drink and murmured wistfully, "Hopefully they can have the kind of life I had envisioned for us. Don't let me get gloomy. I thought we'd have the wedding out here. We could do the grounds beautifully. I thought the ceremony could be done under the weeping spruce tree. The branches hang down creating a natural cathedral."

"Have you ever read a book called *Impossible for Man*?" he asked her.

"No. Why? I never heard of it. Who's it by?"

"No, someone told me it was interesting." Baum could tell by her reaction she was not a party to her son's dishonesty.

"He wants to live out here," Connie said. "I was thinking, how about the Gunderson house? It may come up for sale. Wouldn't it be great to have them live down the road to watch their children grow up? I'm too young to be a grandparent. What am I saying? I'm drunk. Thane's found love. I'm sure if you got to know Sam better, you'd love her too.

I'm sure if you were young she'd have been right up your alley. But you get on well with her. If only you weren't so damn jealous of Thane."

They had almost gotten through a conversation without bitterness, but Asher was too exhausted to bite.

"I understand Thane is working on a new novel," he said.

"He is. He's torn because he's gotten some offers to teach or be an artist in residence. They all want young people. I don't know, but he's of two minds about this book he's working on. You have to ask him. I'll bet he'd make a wonderful teacher. He's got a winning way."

"Well, I'm a little beat. I'm going to turn in."

"There's cold chicken in the kitchen."

"I'm not hungry," Baum said and left Connie with her miniseries. He took a glass of cold water, drank it, and then headed up the stairs. He wanted to shower but didn't dare lest he miss a call from Sam. He had not heard from her and felt she must have finished the book or enough of it by now to see the egregious theft, the kidnapping of another man's text. He did not have her phone number and didn't want to ask Connie and raise questions. "Why do you need Sam's phone number?" she'd ask.

Guilt, that powerful enveloping element as prevalent as oxygen and perhaps as necessary. Still, he was nervous she hadn't called. But why should he feel guilty? He wasn't the criminal in this heist. Thane is the guy the authorities should have the bloodhounds after.

"Why the hell hasn't she called?" Baum said.

"She probably hasn't finished it," he replied.

"She doesn't have to read the whole book to come face-to-face with the crime."

"So she read some and got drowsy and she'll call you in the morning."

"I told her to call the minute she finished it."

"Maybe she read it and doesn't agree," he told himself.

"What are you kidding me? How can she not agree? It's such a blatant theft. You read it, right?"

"Sure I read it."

"So am I crazy? Am I making too much of it?"

"No. He plagiarized it. And not small parts. Big sections, the idea, the characters."

"Precisely and plagiarism is a crime, isn't it?"

"Copyright infringement is."

"How do you know?"

"I looked it up."

"You did?"

"Don't you remember? Yes. If he's made money stealing this book and he's made plenty, he could get a fine."

"Yes. And up to fifteen years in jail."

"Okay, so you know."

"I don't want to see him go to jail. But she should know who she's marrying. Now I'm sorry I said anything."

"You were drunk. You were flirting with someone who reminds you of Tyler."

"I don't know if I can go to sleep until she calls."

Truer words were never said. Baum kept waiting and waiting, tired eyes, heavy lids, and yet he couldn't fall asleep. And she never called. Hypochondriac that he was, it crossed his mind she was so shaken by the crude pillage and what lay in store for the man she hoped to marry that she ended it all. Sleeping pills. No way. Or maybe gas. Head in the stove. Baum drifted in and out of sleep. Finally dawn but no call from Sam. Connie rose early and went for a run to work off the night's booze. While she was out Baum went through her cell phone to filch Sam's number. It wasn't there. He tried tiptoeing into Thane's room to get it and got caught.

"What are you doing?"

"I was looking for Sam's phone number. I drove her into the city yesterday and lost something. I wondered if she found it?"

"What'd you lose?"

"What?"

"What'd you lose?"

"A small manila envelope." Baum, a poor liar, sweated and mumbled as he lied.

"Here, I'll get her for you," Thane said, dialing his cell phone.

"Oh, don't bother, you're sick."

"You won't catch anything. I'm much better." Thane dialed. Long pause.

Baum nervous, standing, shifting his balance back and forth as he waited. She won't know what I'm talking about if I have to tell her about a manila envelope, he thought. But why should I be nervous? I didn't steal anybody's novel. I once set a story in Prague because it was Kafkaesque. But I didn't plagiarize anything.

No answer. "Hi babe, it's me. Call me back when you get a chance. Asher seems to have lost a manila envelope. If you've seen it."

He thanked Thane who turned over in bed to grab another half hour or so before meeting the world.

What's wrong? Where the hell could she be? Did she wait till the morning to start the book and still be locked away reading it? I'm jumping out of my skin.

"What time did Sam say she was coming back?" Connie asked before showering.

"She didn't," he said, certain that something was very wrong. The morning passed and Baum's anxiety level was ready to reach escape velocity. She was unreachable by phone and did not return messages. Connie spent the remainder of the morning on the phone with friends making plans to catch a fashion exhibition in Manhattan the following week and also telling them the good news, that Thane's agent was discussing a very big movie deal for his book and that he and Samantha Taylor had decided to marry around Thanksgiving. Thane had made notes for another book, she told them, and might opt for a residency at a very prestigious college. She wouldn't give away the name.

Baum accosted Thane after he awoke on two occasions, rare for Baum, and causing suspicion toward Baum's deep concern for this mysterious manila envelope. Once Baum asked if he had heard from Sam and Thane said no and that she undoubtedly had some meetings to go to. She always had meetings, although Baum had called her office and she hadn't come in today. No explanation. My god, is she dead in her apartment? Meanwhile Baum was trying over and over to get up the nerve to ask Thane if he had ever read a book called *Impossible for Man* and see his reaction. No matter how hard he tried, he could not go through with it. They were all on the front lawn when a hired car pulled up, the door opened and out stepped Sam.

She was frazzled, bloodshot, not the same Sam. She held a copy of *Impossible for Man* in her hand, walked up to Thane and threw the book at his feet.

"What's going on?" Connie said, taken aback by the gesture.

"Ask him," Sam said.

"Where did you find this book?" Thane said.

"Your stepfather found it in an out-of-print bookstore. He read it and when I told him we were planning to marry, he felt I should know about it."

"What's going on?" Connie repeated. "What is this?"

"What's going on is your son's novel, the one that brought him all this hoopla and adulation, not to mention dollars, he stole outright."

"What are you talking about?" Connie said.

"Ask Thane. He can give you the whole story," Sam said angrily.

"What is this all about Thane? I don't understand," Connie said.

Thane stood there too dumbfounded to speak.

"Forgive me for being blunt but your son stole another man's book, thought he could get away with it and did for a while till Asher brought the book to my attention and the whole disgusting scheme unraveled."

"Is this so, Thane?" Connie asked. "You plagiarized your book? I don't believe it."

"Why is everyone getting so overheated?" Thane said. "I came across an obscure, out-of-print book, a totally over-looked book, from the last century that resonated with some ideas I already had plus some great characters. All wasted, in this novel practically nobody had read. The writer was dead, the publishing house had long ago gone under and the plot and characters had never gotten any real exposure. The theme was picture perfect for a modern-day story I had in mind, much more relevant now than when this came out. No harm was done. Not to the author, the publisher or any descendants of which there are none because I checked. Obviously, no one has said anything, and I was sure no one would know or care. And no one did till this character, who is trying to sabotage me, made an issue of it with Sam."

"I read the book last night," Sam said. "It was clear what a theft this was after fifty pages. But I finished it, and I was so stunned I called Henry Cobb at midnight and told him. I thought he'd die. He told me to bring it right over. To bring it at midnight. This morning he was finished with you."

"He's in no trouble. We should just move on," Thane said.

"Are you kidding?" Sam said. "Then you don't know Henry Cobb. You think he's going to go on publishing your book and not expose the truth? Then you don't know Henry. He trusted you. The deceit, the calculated immorality, his reputation as a publisher, as a man of integrity. You betrayed him. This morning he called his press people and publicly disavowed any knowledge of the original source. He's apologized and halted publication."

"I don't believe this," Connie said. "Is Cobb crazy?"

"On the subject of honesty and integrity I'd hardly call him crazy."

"Henry's problem is he's too intense," Thane said.

Now Connie, who was terribly white with shock, began turning scarlet, her rage rising as she stared at Baum.

"Why did you do this?"

"What?" he said unable to close the Pandora's box he had opened trying to do a good thing.

"You stupid fool," she continued, "and the truth is you're not stupid. You're malicious."

"What'd I do? The kid stole the book and you're getting mad at me?"

"It was all going so smoothly. No one said anything. Okay, he did wrong, but the book was out of print, the publisher gone, the writer dead, no heirs. Did you have to open your goddamn mouth? Was there no other way to handle it? No one might have ever said anything if you hadn't made an issue of it."

"An issue?" Baum said. "His publisher is the one making it into a major deal. I just told Sam. Since she was marrying Thane, I thought she should know."

"What business of it is yours that he and Sam were marrying?" Connie said.

"I felt she should know what she was getting into."

"Who are you, her guardian?"

"I thought about the morality—what would Kant do?"

"Don't lay this off on Kant, you slimy weasel. You're a snitch. Now everybody knows or will by tomorrow. The press, the scandal, the disgrace." Tears were forming in Connie's eyes, tears of rage and humiliation, tears reaching two hundred and twelve degrees Fahrenheit. "You've ruined his life," Connie said, also through clenched teeth.

Baum, at that moment was so sorry he had ever run into the roach man, sorry he found out, read the book and warned the girl, sorry that he'd awakened that morning, lived on the earth, was a meaningless agglomeration of cells killing time between one abyss and another.

What's with Baum?

"This will be all over the press," Connie said, "but it needn't have been. The whole thing could have passed unnoticed. It could have been resolved privately. You could have had a one-on-one talk with him, explained to him this was unacceptable and he should never ever do anything like it again. You're his stepfather, not his rival for this girl's affection. You fancied Sam."

"What are you talking about? You're out of control, Connie," Baum said, gesticulating with his free hand while the other was firmly now trapped in the cookie jar. "I only told Sam. She told Cobb. Cobb went bananas."

"Now he will be reviled as a plagiarist. It will be in every paper, not just the tabloids."

"Sam," Thane said, getting the message loud and clear there would be no wedding come Thanksgiving, or any time after in perpetuity.

"Where are you going?" Connie said to Sam as she hurried to the house.

"To get what I left here and back to the city."

The limo driver now approached them. He was Mr. Perry Brodnax, slightly pudgy with a sweet face. "Is there a bathroom I could use?" he said.

Sam had marched to the house to retrieve her belongings and to walk out of Thane's life. Thane followed pleading his case.

"This is an egregious rush to judgment," he said. But who could explain such a sleazy business.

Connie stared at Baum. "You see what you've done? You insect, you termite. His career, his marriage."

"Is there a bathroom I could use?" the driver reiterated.

"Shut up," Connie screamed at him and ran to the house in tears.

"What'd you do so terrible?" the driver asked Baum.

"There's a bathroom right there by the pool house," he said.

"What did I do?" Baum asked himself.

"You're a whistleblower," he answered. "They always catch flack."

"Should I have not said anything? Then she married this phony and goes through hell. If he cheated with this book he could cheat on her."

"I don't know what the details are," the limo driver said, "but in those prison movies the squealer always comes off bad."

"Who the hell asked you?" Baum said.

"Weren't you talking to me?" the driver said. "There's no one else here."

"You wanted a bathroom," Baum said pointing again.

"I'm sorry," the driver said confused and hurried off in the direction Baum indicated.

"Help me," Baum said. "I'm coming apart."

"There is no justice. Maybe in an alternate universe but with your luck I wouldn't count on it even there."

And now, as if a director had staged it, Connie came storming out of the house with a pistol. My god, where did

Connie get a pistol? The first thought that went through Baum's mind was she was going to kill herself, but the second more precise observation was that she intended to shoot him. She took careful aim and fired. A wild miss. Baum recalled when she talked of buying a gun. Of how safe she said the country was. And yet she wanted to buy a gun. The idea terrified him and he made her promise she would not do it. She said if it bothered him so much she wouldn't. She had been lying, and not only did she have a gun but was now aiming it at him and blasting away.

He took off and ran to the woods hoping to lose himself amongst the trees. Connie chasing him, firing a few times, missing her target but getting closer. Baum bounded through the thicket, the trees, the bushes, thinking how much he'd prefer to be running down Fifty-Seventh Street or up Third Avenue where he was at one with the terrain. Meanwhile he huffed and puffed over dirt and grass and snapping the dried twigs as the seriousness of the situation became more apparent when she stopped to reload.

"See shmuck," he told himself breathlessly, "this is what it's all come to. Running for your life through bramble from an overwrought woman who's got a target on your back."

"What'd I do? She's crazy."

"She's crazy and you're crazy. The only difference is she's armed."

A bullet grazed his neck and a drop of blood trickled on his Banana Republic T-shirt. "My god, my wife is going to kill me," he rasped. He didn't want to die. To be hunted down like game in the woods. Nor did he want to be run through with a Samurai sword on the Staten Island Ferry. The truth was, for all his whining about the awful cosmos and the pointlessness of life, he wanted to live. "And don't ask me why," he said.

Out of breath he came to a clearing. It was the highway. He kept running till he was in the middle. Cars whizzed by. Connie came to the edge of the woods and gave up the chase, her ammunition spent. Cars stopped, seeing him waving his arms in distress.

"She's trying to kill me," he said.

"Okay," he told himself, "you're okay."

"Who are all these people? Why is traffic stopping?"

"They're here to help you," he said.

"I don't need help. What the hell did I do?"

Now drivers bogged down in a traffic jam, horrified while a lunatic ran wild and a trooper's car pulled up.

"What's going on here?"

"What is going on?" Baum asked. "Are they stopping for me? Are all these cars for me?"

"Yes," he answered himself. "Pull yourself together. You're embarrassing me."

The trooper said, "Take it easy. Just relax. Calm down. We'll take care of you."

"Listen to him Asher," he said to himself. "You're coming apart."

What's with Baum?

"Get him off my back," Baum said to the trooper. "He used to be easy to get along with. Lately he's gotten snide. And I don't like it. I don't appreciate snide."

In a film this would be a fade-out as the troopers patiently tried to calm Baum down. Go to black and then fade up weeks later and Baum is talking to his brother at a very lovely rehab center. It is rural but he doesn't seem to mind. There are other patients with problems worse than his. In fact, he is leaving today after six weeks. The two men talk as Josh helps Baum pack his suitcase.

"Your room's all set," Josh says. "You'll stay with me till you get back on your feet again, and there is no rush."

"I won't be staying long. I feel so much better."

"You look good, Asher. Your color's back. You're not ranting anymore, babbling into thin air."

"And what news of the outside world?"

"Well, you know Connie filed for divorce. She and Thane are over in England with his birth father. More than that, I have no big news. Believe me you didn't miss anything. You needed rest. Be thankful you weren't around for the tabloid feeding frenzy. You, Connie with the gun, Thane with all the terrible publicity. Oh, and some Japanese journalist who accused you of grabbing her. What the hell was that all about? Christ, you'd think you had her chained in the basement. If I were you I'd come away with me. Did I tell you I'm taking a boat down the Amazon? Get away from civilization for a while."

"Sounds great. Snakes, headhunters. Just my thing."

"Don't forget the quicksand."

"No, I think I'll stay in New York and take my chances here. I plan to get to work on a new book."

"Good idea. You're always best when you're working. Incidentally, I asked a friend about digging up Papa and it's actually not as big a to-do as I thought."

The two men finished packing and exited the building, walking across the lawn to Josh's car.

"Got an idea already for a new book?" he asked Baum.

"I do."

"Want to share it?"

"You really want to hear it?"

"I do."

"It's twenty billion years in the future. Existence is over. There's nothing. No universe. No stars, no light, no space, no time. Absolute nothing."

"And what happens?"

"I haven't figured that part out yet."

Baum got into the passenger seat next to his brother, and they pulled out.